A Little House
of Their Own

The CAROLINE *Years*
By Maria D. Wilkes and Celia Wilkins
Illustrated by Dan Andreasen

A Little House of Their Own

Celia Wilkins

Illustrations by Dan Andreasen

HarperCollins*Publishers*

HarperCollins®, ☕®, Little House®, and The Caroline Years™
are trademarks of HarperCollins Publishers Inc.

Library of Congress Cataloging-in-Publication Data
Wilkins, Celia.
    A little house of their own / Celia Wilkins ; illustrations by Dan
Andreasen.— 1st ed.
        p.   cm.— (Little house)
    "The Caroline years."
    Summary: After achieving her dream of becoming a teacher in her
small farm town of Concord, Wisconsin, in 1857, seventeen-year-old
Caroline Quiner, who will become the mother of Laura Ingalls Wilder,
begins a courtship with Charles Ingalls, a bachelor farmer who aspires to
move west.
    ISBN 0-06-027009-8 — ISBN 0-06-440736-5 (pbk.)
    1. Ingalls, Caroline Lake Quiner—Juvenile fiction. [1. Ingalls,
Caroline Lake Quiner—Fiction. 2. Wilder, Laura Ingalls 1867–1957—
Family—Fiction. 3. Teachers—Fiction. 4. Courtship—Fiction. 5. Farm
life—Wisconsin—Fiction. 6. Wisconsin—History—19th century—
Fiction.] I. Andreasen, Dan, ill. II. Title. III. Series.
PZ7.W648498Lk 2005   2004010141
[Fic]—dc22   CIP
                                                                AC

1   2   3   4   5   6   7   8   9   10
❖
First Edition

*The author wishes to thank Amy Edgar Sklansky for her
excellent research; Kimberly Neuhaus and Kedin Kilgore for
offering a quiet place to work; Tara Weikum and Alix Reid for
their perseverance; Renée Cafiero for her diligence; Melissa
Peterson for her knowledge of all things Scottish and Little
House; and Tim Ungs for his patience.*

Author's Note

Many years before she ever put pen to paper to create what would become the Little House books, Laura Ingalls Wilder wrote to her aunt Martha Quiner Carpenter, and asked her to "tell the story of those days" when she and Laura's mother, Caroline, were young girls. Laura's mother had never talked much about her childhood in the newly settled Wisconsin territory, and so Aunt Martha wrote several letters to Laura filled with memories of the Quiners' day-to-day life during the 1840s and 1850s. These letters became the basis for the Caroline series.

Through the letters and through careful research, I came to understand that times were not always easy for young Caroline and her family. There were years of hardship after the sudden, tragic death of Caroline's father—years in which Caroline learned firsthand what it took to survive in a vast and sometimes unforgiving wilderness. It took courage and resilience and an indomitable pioneer spirit— the very traits Caroline would pass on to her own daughters after she had grown up and married another child of the western frontier, Charles Ingalls.

In A Little House of Their Own, *I have sought to present the most realistic portrait possible of Caroline Quiner's life as a girl and young woman, while striving to stay true to Laura's own depiction of her beloved Ma in the Little House books.*

—*C.W.*

Contents

Miss Quiner

"Wake up, Miss Quiner!" a voice whispered, pulling Caroline out of a deep, dream-filled sleep. "Wouldn't do for the schoolteacher to be late on the first day of school!"

Caroline gasped and sat straight up in bed. Had she really overslept? Frantically she glanced about the room she shared with her two sisters.

No, the light filtering through the glass windowpanes was still just a soft glow. At that very moment, the rooster gave his cheerful morning call from his perch in the barnyard.

Cock-a-doodle-doo!

Caroline fell back into her goose-down pillow with a relieved sigh. She had been dreaming that she was still a little girl and she had lost something precious in the woods. She could not find it no matter how hard she searched. The dream had seemed so real, but of course she was not a little girl. She was seventeen years old. It was May 4, 1857, the day she would begin her new life as a schoolteacher at Concord School.

"Good morning, Miss Quiner!" Eliza called in a singsong, leaning in close to grin at Caroline as she rubbed the sleep out of her eyes.

Caroline reached out and gently yanked one of the blond braids that had escaped from Eliza's white cotton nightcap. "Don't tease the teacher or you'll have to stay in at recess!" she scolded with a smile.

"Yes, Miss Quiner," Eliza replied, giggling.

"Miss Quiner, hah!" Martha's sleepy voice rose up from her side of the big bed. "I'm glad I'm through with school so I don't have to call my own sister Miss Quiner. I just don't think I could do it!"

"I don't mind," Eliza said, shrugging. "It will be so nice to have you as the teacher instead of Skinny Linney."

"Oh, goodness, don't call him that!" Caroline sat up again and stretched the sleep out of her limbs. "I hate to think of scholars calling Mr. Linney names. I would feel awful if someone called me names behind my back."

"Someone probably will," mumbled Martha.

"Oh, Martha!" Caroline turned to glance at her older sister. Martha was lying still, eyes closed tight against the morning light. She always liked to stay in bed as long as she possibly could.

"Moody Martha, you mean!" Eliza whispered, nudging Caroline.

Ever since she was a little girl, Martha had been cranky in the morning. Even though she was a young lady of nineteen—and engaged to boot—she was still "Moody Martha," and

Caroline tried not to pay her grumblings before breakfast too much mind.

"They will probably call you snooty," Martha said, yawning and rubbing her eyes open at last.

"Why would they call me that?" Caroline asked, surprised.

"Because you went away to college in the big city and came back with all your fancy clothes," Martha answered.

It was true that Caroline had attended college in the city of Milwaukee, and it was also true that she had returned with two beautiful dresses her aunt Jane and uncle Elisha had bought for her, and new shoes and gloves as well. Still, she didn't think these things made her snooty. She felt a pang of guilt, knowing that Martha probably spoke out of jealousy. She remembered the look of envy on Martha's face when she had first returned from Milwaukee with her new things.

"Don't listen to her," Eliza whispered now. "She's just being her grumpy self. I feel sorry for Charlie, don't you?"

Charlie Carpenter was Martha's sweetheart from way back in Brookfield, and now he was her betrothed. They planned to wed as soon as Charlie had saved enough money.

"Moody Martha might have to change her ways when she is a married lady, or she'll scare poor Charlie away!" Eliza said. Then she shrieked and scrambled out of bed to escape Martha's pinching fingers, landing with a loud thump on the floor.

"Girls, is something wrong?" Mother's concerned voice rose up from the kitchen below.

Caroline and Eliza and Martha glanced at one another and answered in unison, "No, ma'am."

"Very well, then, don't tarry. The morning's a-wasting," Mother called.

"Yes, ma'am," the girls answered again, then burst into laughter.

How lovely it was to wake up with sisters— even if one was moody, Caroline thought as she washed her hands and face in the china washbasin on the dresser. The nine months spent in Milwaukee had been exciting, but she had also been lonely at times. Caroline had had her very own room with her very own bed in her uncle's large house. She had been grateful for the luxury, but she knew now that she preferred the crowded coziness of home.

Once she had graduated from Milwaukee Female College and returned to Concord, she had hoped to find a nearby school to teach, but this had proved impossible. So she had gone back to her old school, helping Mr. Linney with the younger scholars and trying not to feel discouraged. But the longer she went without real employment, the guiltier she felt about the money Mother and Pa had spent to send her away to college in the first place.

At last she had received an offer from the school board in Elm Grove. The tiny town was raising a school, and it would be ready for the summer term. Elm Grove was a two-day drive from Concord, which meant she would have to board with a family there. Caroline hated the idea of living so far from home again, but of course she could not refuse the job on account of being homesick. She had been just about to accept the post when something miraculous happened.

Mr. Linney had abruptly given his notice. He had inherited a large sum of money from a distant relative back east. Suddenly he was a man of leisure, and Caroline had promptly been hired to teach Concord School.

Caroline could hardly believe her good fortune. Not only would she be a real teacher, earning the handsome sum of twenty dollars per term, she would be teaching at her very own school, the school she had attended for years. Best of all, she would not have to leave home.

"Aren't you nervous to be in charge of school all by yourself?" Martha asked, interrupting Caroline's thoughts. "You're only seventeen, after all. Mighty young to be a teacher. Mr. Linney is old—twenty-five at least."

"I *am* seventeen and a half," Caroline replied as she changed out of her nightgown and into her good chemise.

Caroline helped Eliza with the stays of her

corset and waited while Eliza returned the favor. After the corset was laced about her slim waist, she slipped into her best petticoat, the one with the lace trim she had tatted herself. Next came the stiff crinoline to make her skirt flare out like a perfect round bell.

"Oh, well!" Martha said laughingly. "That half makes all the difference in the world!"

"It doesn't matter how old I am anyway," Caroline said. "I have wanted to be a teacher for a long time. I'm not nervous in the least."

As soon as the words were spoken, however, Caroline realized they weren't entirely true. She *was* nervous. Her insides were aflutter, and her hands trembled slightly, fingers fumbling with the tiny buttons of her blue serge dress.

Turning to face her own reflection in the round mirror that hung above the dresser, Caroline told herself that what she was feeling was perfectly normal. She had loved school from a very early age, but first days always made her jittery—nervous and worried and excited all at once. It was only natural that she would feel the same thing on her very first day as teacher.

Even so, she was glad when Eliza offered to fix her hair, as she often did on special occasions. Caroline wasn't sure she trusted her own trembling fingers, and Eliza's tiny hands were particularly good at twisting and braiding and pinning.

"Your hair is so lovely, even if it is only brown," Eliza teased as she undid Caroline's single long braid from the night before and brushed it out.

"We can't all have blond curls like you," Caroline retorted.

"Yes, but my hair is so very fine, it doesn't seem to grow." Eliza sighed. "Yours and Martha's is so thick and long! Look! It's down to your knees now!" She let Caroline's hair hang loose, and indeed it did fall nearly to the back of Caroline's knees.

"Long thick hair is all the more trouble to wash," Martha grumbled.

Once a month on a Saturday evening the girls washed their hair, and then they had to sit by the fire for hours doing their mending or schoolwork, waiting for it to dry.

"Sometimes I think I'd like to cut off all my hair and sell it," Martha announced as she came to stand beside Caroline at the mirror. "I hear Mr. Jayson pays good money at the general store for hair."

"What does he do with it?" Eliza asked, wide-eyed.

"He sends it off to Milwaukee to have wigs made, of course," Martha replied matter-of-factly.

"Martha, what would Charlie think if you didn't have any hair!" Eliza cried, beginning to giggle again.

Caroline couldn't help but laugh a little as well. It made an amusing picture, imagining Martha with shorn hair like a sheep in spring.

"I could wear a wig like Widow Milton does," Martha answered, taking up the comb and smoothing down her hair without bothering to rebraid it. Briskly she wound the braid into a heavy knot at the nape of her neck and pinned it.

"Widow Milton wears a wig?" Eliza asked, eyes wide again.

Martha nodded. "And wooden teeth too. I have to cook soft things for her—otherwise she can't eat a bite. She likes puddings best of all."

Eliza let out a peal of laughter again, but this time Caroline did not join in. She did not think it was right to laugh at anyone's expense. Widow Milton was old and all alone in the world, and besides, she was Martha's employer. The widow paid Martha a dollar fifty a week to do her cleaning and cooking and to keep her company in the afternoons now that Martha no longer went to school.

"Martha, I don't think you should gossip about Widow Milton," Caroline said sternly.

Martha glanced at herself in the mirror and smoothed her hair and skirt and said in a curt voice, "We can't all be as good as you, *Miss Quiner*!" With that, she turned on her heel and left the room.

Caroline sighed. She hadn't meant to hurt Martha's feelings. "I'm not really so good," she said in a quiet voice.

"Yes, you are. But that is why we love you," Eliza answered lightly, giving Caroline's shoulders a quick squeeze. "Now sit still so I can finish your hair!" she commanded.

"Yes, ma'am," Caroline answered.

As she waited for Eliza to work her magic, humming gaily all the while, Caroline thought about how different her sisters could be. Martha had always been quick-tempered and stubborn, while Eliza's nature was more pliable and sweet. Caroline knew herself to be somewhere in the middle of the two. Martha often accused Caroline of being too good, as if it were something to be ashamed of. Caroline did strive to be as good and patient as she could be in all situations, but she didn't think she always succeeded.

"There! Just as you like it!" Eliza said, stepping back to admire her handiwork.

"Oh, Eliza, it's perfect," Caroline cried. She took up the little hand mirror to look at her hair from all sides.

Eliza had parted her hair straight down the

middle and looped the sides smoothly down
to cover her ears. The back was coiled into a
lovely French twist. Caroline had begun to
wear her hair this way last year in Milwaukee,
when a maid had actually helped her dress in
the morning. Eliza had copied the style perfectly.

"Thank you, Eliza!" Caroline breathed.

"You're quite welcome," Eliza replied.

Now Caroline hurried to finish dressing.
She pulled on the stockings she had knitted
herself and stepped into the beautiful black
leather ankle boots Aunt Jane had bought for
her in Milwaukee.

"I'm glad I don't have to wear stockings
and shoes—even if they are pretty ones!"
Eliza said, scrunching up her nose. "It's only
May, but it feels like summer already."

Caroline gave a little shrug. "It wouldn't do
for the schoolteacher to go barefoot."

"I guess not. But don't you hate it?" Eliza
asked.

"Actually, no," Caroline said. She had
gotten used to wearing shoes all year round in

Milwaukee. Perhaps Martha would say it was evidence of her being snooty, but after she had returned home, it had felt odd to go barefoot.

"I guess you're grown up," Eliza said, sighing.

"I guess so," Caroline replied, feeling a little strange as she said it. She gave a final glance at the mirror. Instead of wearing one of the fancier Milwaukee dresses, she had chosen to wear the dress Mother had made for her when she went away to college. The blue serge with its black velvet trim was more appropriate for a first day of school. It was fashionable, but not too fancy.

"You look so pretty. Just like a lady teacher should look," Eliza said approvingly.

"Thank you, Eliza!" Caroline said.

Downstairs, Mother was standing at the stove, busily flipping hotcakes on the griddle.

"How's our schoolteacher this morning?" she asked, smiling at Caroline.

"Fine, thank you, Mother." Caroline tied on her big apron and looked about to see what there was to do, but it seemed that everything was nearly ready. Martha had brought in the water from the well, and the table was already set.

"I carried the plates all by myself!" Lottie cried proudly, rushing up to Caroline.

"What a good helper you are!" Caroline said, leaning down to give her little sister a kiss on the forehead.

Lottie was only three years old, the newest member of the family. She was small and fair, with enormous blue eyes. The whole family spoiled her terribly because she was the only baby left. Everyone else was nearly grown.

Joseph and Henry were over twenty now. They were bachelor farmers, living in a little cabin on a plot of land at the edge of Mother and Pa's. They had purchased the plot with money saved from hauling lumber for other farmers. They still helped Pa with the planting and harvesting, but they were always busy, and Caroline seemed to hardly see them anymore.

Thomas was the only boy left at home. He

was thirteen, and a great help to Pa on the farm. He came into the kitchen now, carrying the milk pails from the morning's milking, and started to hand them to Martha, but Caroline intervened.

"I'll take them, Martha, since you got the water and did the sweeping," Caroline said in a cheerful voice. She wanted to somehow let Martha know that she hadn't meant to hurt her feelings before.

Caroline took the milk pails into the pantry and poured half the milk into a jug to put on the kitchen table and half into milk tins to wait for Martha when she did the churning later that morning.

"Breakfast is ready!" Mother called, setting the platter of hotcakes on the table.

Eliza came in from seeing to the hens and geese, and then Pa arrived, limping a little. Unlike the rest of the family, he had never seemed to fully recover from his bout with cholera years before. His legs were often achy and sore.

"Here we are, boarding the schoolteacher

again," he said, giving Caroline an approving nod. "And I reckon we're glad to do it, too!"

When Caroline had been a young girl, they had boarded Miss May, a teacher who had come all the way from New York State to teach Concord School. Caroline had always liked school, but it was Miss May who had truly inspired her to become a teacher.

After the blessing they all ate quickly. Everyone was in a hurry that morning. Pa and Thomas were in the middle of planting, and Caroline had to be at the schoolhouse early to tidy up.

As they were nearly done eating, Ma gazed down the length of the table at Caroline. "I can hardly believe how grown you are, Caroline! How grown all my girls are!"

"Am I grown?" Lottie asked, with such a surprised expression that everyone at the table laughed.

"You've got a ways to go yet," Pa said, reaching out to tug on Lottie's pointed chin. Pa had married Mother eight years before, five years after Caroline's own father had died when his trader's ship capsized in a storm. Pa had always treated Caroline and her sisters like daughters, but Caroline knew Lottie held a special place in his heart, since she was his very own.

After breakfast, Caroline packed the dinner pail she would share with Eliza at noon. She sliced the thick brown bread from Saturday's baking and smeared the slices with creamy butter. Mother gave her two pieces of salt pork left over from breakfast. As a special treat, there were two pieces of gingerbread.

She slipped into the little casaque jacket that matched her dress and tied on her good straw bonnet with new silk flowers trimming the brim. Then she picked up her leather satchel.

"I'll carry the dinner pail," Eliza offered, reaching for it.

"Teacher's pet," Martha called from where she was wiping the breakfast dishes, but when she caught Caroline's eye, she was smiling. "Good luck, Caroline," she said.

"Thank you, Martha!" Caroline answered,

and then she bent down to give Lottie a kiss good-bye.

Mother followed her out into the yard, wiping her hands on her apron. "I am so proud of you, Caroline," she said. "You are a schoolteacher now. And I know your father would have been very proud to see you today."

"Thank you, Mother!" Caroline exclaimed. "Thank you for everything. I promise I will work hard to pay you back for putting me through college."

Mother's eyes sparkled in the morning sun. "You already have, my dear," she said, and then she squeezed Caroline's arm and went back into the house.

Caroline took a deep breath, then turned to walk with Eliza the two miles to Concord School.

Summer School

Sunlight filtered prettily through the green leaves as Caroline and Eliza made their way along the worn footpath through the woods. The lark and thrush trilled their happy morning songs and darted among the branches high overhead. A woodpecker hammered busily at a tree somewhere close by. The crickets clicked in the tall grasses all around.

As she walked, Caroline reached into her skirt pocket. The key to the schoolhouse was tucked inside. She held it tightly for a moment, smiling to herself, and let it go again.

"Do you think it will be strange to teach your friends?" Eliza asked.

Caroline had thought about this a great deal during the past few weeks. Of course she would be friendly during school hours, but she would need to be somewhat reserved as well. "I will treat everyone exactly the same. Fair and square."

"No favorites?" Eliza asked.

"Of course not," Caroline replied.

"Aren't you scared—just a little? You can tell me now that we're alone."

"I guess I am a bit nervous," Caroline answered truthfully. "It will be nice to begin with summer school before I have to teach a larger group."

Summer school was for girls of all ages and for the younger boys who did not have to help their families with the planting. The term lasted three months: May, June, and July. Caroline would have all of August to help around the farm and to prepare for teaching again in the fall and winter, when the school would be more crowded.

As Caroline and Eliza came out of the woods, the leafy shade gave way to bright sunshine. The wide Territorial Road that led into the town of Concord was already bustling with horses and wagons—farmers on their way to the mill or the general store or some other place of business. The men waved or nodded good morning to the girls as they jingled by. One young man they didn't know tipped his hat and smiled broadly.

"Morning, ladies!" he called in a cheerful voice from atop his wagon.

"Morning," Caroline and Eliza answered together.

"He was handsome," Eliza whispered, giggling, after the driver was out of earshot. "There are so many bachelor farmers around here now!"

"How do you know he's a bachelor?" Caroline asked.

"He has that same hungry look that Joseph and Henry have," Eliza said. "They all want a wife to cook their meals for them. Maybe you'll get engaged like Martha, and you won't have to teach school."

"But I want to teach school!" Caroline protested.

"I'd rather keep house," Eliza said wistfully.

"Oh, Eliza, you're only fifteen!" Caroline cried. "You shouldn't think about that yet."

"Nell Spivey married last year, and she was only sixteen and a half," Eliza said.

"True," Caroline replied thoughtfully. Nell was a good friend of Martha's. Last year she had married her sweetheart, Jacob Graylick, and they already had a baby boy. Caroline knew that one day she wanted a husband and a house and a family of her own, but she also knew that she didn't want to marry as quickly as Nell had. She wanted to be a schoolteacher for a few years yet. Besides, getting married so soon would be a waste of her good education and of the money Mother and Pa had scraped together to send her away to college.

As the girls got closer to town, the woods on either side of Territorial Road disappeared completely and gave way to cleared farmland. Even though she passed this way nearly every day, it was still a marvel to Caroline how much had changed in such a short time. When her family had first arrived here almost a decade before, they had found very few neighbors. Now the woods and land surrounding Concord were full of settlers. In the half mile leading to town there were at least a dozen houses clustered close together, with split rail fences separating the yards.

The town itself had changed a great deal as well. Instead of one lonely store on Main Street, now there were four: a general store, a blacksmith's, a cooper's shop, and a wagon maker's shed. There was also an inn, a mill, two churches, and of course the school.

The four shops were built close together and joined by a raised wooden sidewalk. Mr. Jayson, who owned the general store, and Mr. Biles, the blacksmith, were both outside, sweeping the wide planks clean.

"Good morning, young ladies!" they called as Caroline and Eliza passed.

Mr. Kellogg's inn stood at the crossroads. The building was two stories high with a wide, wraparound porch. The planks had been painted a crisp white, and there were red-and-white-checked curtains at the windows. Twice a week the stagecoach stopped here, and travelers paid money to eat and sometimes to stay overnight. On Saturday afternoons the porch was often crowded with men from town playing checkers and talking over the news of the day.

Now Mr. Kellogg himself came through the front door and trotted down the stairs, greeting Caroline and Eliza warmly as he approached.

"Good morning, young ladies!" he said. "I see you are on the way to school. I trust you will find everything in order there, Caroline."

"I am sure that I will, Mr. Kellogg," Caroline replied. "I want to thank you again for giving me this chance."

Mr. Kellogg was the richest man in town, and he was head of the school board. It was Mr. Kellogg who had actually hired Caroline. She had thanked him already, but she didn't think she could ever tell him how grateful she was.

"Well, I am pleased that you are to be the schoolteacher, Caroline," Mr. Kellogg said, and then he let out a short laugh. "Why, I remember when you were just a little thing, new to Concord, and you were already pestering me to build a school."

Caroline's cheeks warmed at the memory. When she and her family had first arrived in Concord, there hadn't been any school at all. One day she had overheard Mr. Kellogg telling Mother about his plans to make Concord a real town. Caroline had hoped his plans included building a school, and she had impertinently told him so.

"Well, I won't keep you now," Mr. Kellogg continued. "I know you are eager to get settled this morning. I wish you well on your first day, Caroline."

"Thank you, Mr. Kellogg!" Caroline answered.

Now the girls turned left at the crossroads and followed the road until they came to a trail. This led through a small patch of woods into a wide-open clearing dotted with tree stumps. The schoolhouse stood in the middle of the clearing, a trim structure built of wide pine planks with a high, pointed roof and tall glass windows.

The words *Concord School* had been painted in bold black letters on a polished piece of wood that hung over the front door.

Caroline paused for a moment at the bottom of the stairs, gazing up at the building. She knew Concord School was small and plain compared to many schools, but at that moment it seemed like a castle.

"Did you forget the key?" Eliza asked, giving Caroline a puzzled look.

"No, no." Caroline laughed and hurried up the steps. Her fingers trembled a little with excitement as she worked the lock and pushed open the heavy pine door.

Inside the entryway it was cool and shadowy. Caroline paused to remove her jacket and bonnet and hang them on the teacher's peg.

"Isn't it strange to put your things there?" Eliza asked. Caroline nodded.

Carefully she smoothed her hair and skirt and took up her satchel again. Briskly she walked through the entryway into the main room, breathing in the distinctive smell of school. It was a mixture of the aging pine walls and a hint of chalk and ink left over from last term, topped off with linseed oil, which was used to polish the desks. The scent made Caroline feel very much at home.

Sunlight streamed through the tall glass windows on two sides of the room, gleaming across the neat rows of pinewood desks. The teacher's desk stood at the front on a raised platform. Behind it the pine wall had been painted a shiny black for the blackboard. There were two neat shelves, one holding a dictionary, a book of geography, and a Bible, the other a clock and globe of the world.

"It's just as we left it," Eliza observed.

"Well, we've been gone only two weeks," Caroline replied.

"What can I do to help you?" Eliza asked.

"I don't think you need to do anything this morning," Caroline replied, glancing about. "I'll just do a little dusting and fetch the water."

There was never as much to do to get ready for summer school. In the fall and winter, there would be the firewood to bring in from the shed outside and the stove to tend to.

"Why don't you go ahead and choose your seat, Eliza," Caroline said.

"Yes, ma'am," Eliza answered, giggling a little. "You sound like the teacher already!"

"What do you mean?" Caroline asked in surprise.

"Your voice changed just now. It's more formal."

"I didn't mean to," Caroline said.

"Well, it doesn't matter. We're in school now, and you are the teacher. I guess it will just take a little getting used to."

While Eliza chose a seat on the girls' side of the room, Caroline found the dustrag in the entryway and dusted the books and globe and wound the clock. She swept out the leaves

that had blown in under the door in the entryway. Then she took the bucket out to the well
and rinsed and filled it full of cool water. The
bucket always sat on a little stool near the
teacher's desk, with a tin cup hanging from
the side. The scholars could take a drink anytime they were thirsty.

Now Caroline set about organizing her own
desk. Opening her satchel, she took out the
books she had acquired over the years: three
worn yellow primers, two brown-and-white-
marbled-cover readers, two arithmetic books,
and a history book.

Besides the books there were a dozen quill
pens she had plucked from the geese at home
and sharpened herself, four bottles of home-
made ink, and a handful of notebooks she had
made out of old brown paper saved from trips
to the general store. All these things she had
brought to share with any scholars who did
not have books and pens and paper of their
own.

When everything was in order, she opened
the drawers of her desk, checking to make

sure there were extra slates and pieces of chalk for scholars who needed them.

In the center drawer Caroline found the big black book that held the names and grades of all past scholars. She turned to the last term she had attended and couldn't help but smile when she caught sight of her own name written in Mr. Linney's fine script, and the words "excellent scholar" beside it.

At last Caroline glanced at the clock. It was a quarter to nine—nearly time for school to begin. At that very moment she heard the muffled sound of voices outside. A fluttering started up again, right in her middle. Her hands went cold, and she clasped them together on top of the desk. Eliza gave her an encouraging smile from her seat, and Caroline smiled back.

Then the front door whooshed open and the outside voices grew louder for a moment and mingled with the sound of footsteps and laughter.

"Good morning, Miss Quiner!" two young voices chimed.

It was Margaret Kellogg and Mary Littleton, two of Eliza's good friends.

"Good morning, girls," Caroline answered cheerfully.

Mary and Margaret hurried to take their seats on either side of Eliza, and the three girls began to quietly chatter together like squirrels in the spring.

Another group of girls, younger than Eliza and her friends, arrived next, and they timidly said, "Good morning, Miss Quiner!" as they took their seats near the front.

"Good morning, Car—I mean Miss Quiner," a familiar voice said. It was Polly Ingalls, one of Caroline's very best friends. Her brown eyes danced merrily, and Caroline could tell Polly thought it was amusing to call her "Miss Quiner."

"Good morning, Polly!" Caroline called. "And good morning, Docia!"

"Good morning, Miss Quiner," Docia answered.

Docia was Polly's sister, nearly the same age as Eliza. The Ingallses lived just across the river from Pa and Mother's land. They were all good friends and neighbors, often trading work and visiting with each other's family. There were so many of them, sometimes Caroline lost track.

Besides Polly and Docia, there was an older sister, Lydia, who worked outside the house just as Martha did. The middle boys, Jamie, Hiram, and George, would come to school in the winter. Two older boys, Charlie and Peter, were working land up north somewhere, while Ruby and baby Lansford stayed at home because they were both younger than Lottie.

Four more friends of Caroline's came in together: Maddy Jayson, Elmira Hawkins, Lucy Brown, and Abigail McFarlane.

Maddy was the most fashionably dressed of the group, as usual. She wore a beautiful blue delaine with a wide skirt and short, frothy sleeves. Since her father was Mr. Jayson, the storekeeper, she always wore the prettiest dresses. She gave Caroline a quick little wave and sat next to Polly—in the seat that had once been Caroline's.

For a brief moment, Caroline felt lonely sitting at her teacher's desk. She wanted nothing more than to take her old place beside Polly, and talk and laugh as she had always done. But that was just plain silly. She was the schoolteacher now, and Polly would always be her friend even if she had to maintain a polite distance during school hours.

Caroline glanced at the clock. It was time to ring the bell and bring the school to order. The boys were all outside, playing as long as they could before school started.

Caroline walked briskly down the aisle with the handbell, smiling at the girls as she passed. Outside, a group of boys was playing tag and some were jumping the stumps. As soon as she rang the bell, however, all the boys swarmed toward her. They clomped up the steps, calling out, "Good morning, Miss Quiner!" as they passed.

A Good First Day

There were only about fifteen scholars, just as Caroline had expected for summer school, and nearly all the faces were familiar. Even so, when she stood at the front of the room and saw everyone staring up at her expectantly, her knees suddenly felt weak.

For what seemed like an eternity to Caroline, she remained frozen, unable to think what to do next. Then she felt the bell, solid in her hand. She held it up and rang it again.

"School has begun!" she announced, turning on her heel. At her desk she picked up the black book. "Please answer when I call your name."

As she began to read, her nerves settled. Then a loud *whoomp-bang!* startled her again.

It was the front door opening and slamming shut, followed by a loud clattering of footsteps. The whole room turned to see who would be so tardy on the first day of school.

A small boy stood in the doorway. He wore a stained shirt and patched britches. His black hair hung limp under his cap, and his green eyes were large inside his thin, dirt-smudged face. He appeared utterly surprised to find the whole school staring at him.

The boys in the back row burst into laughter right away, and the youngest girls began to giggle too. The expression on the newcomer's face changed instantly to anger.

"Ah, what are you all laughing at?" the boy asked, scowling.

This caused another fit of laughter.

Caroline had not expected trouble so soon

in the day! She rapped a wooden ruler against her desk.

"Indeed, class, there is nothing to laugh about!" she called. "School has begun! Please face forward."

Fortunately, the laughter died right away and everyone turned back to face the front. Caroline noticed how the new boy's defiant expression melted and a look of pure terror passed over his face. Perhaps he was not trying to cause trouble after all. He was simply scared at being new.

"Young man," Caroline said in a gentle voice, "please remove your cap and come forward."

The boy's green eyes grew suspicious, staring at her. He looked as if he were about to turn and flee.

Caroline smiled and beckoned to him. "You are new here. I need to write your name and age in the book."

Slowly the boy took off his cap and bunched it in his hands. He walked down the aisle, without looking left or right, to stand in front of Caroline's desk.

"Your name, please?" she asked, giving the boy another encouraging smile.

"John Friday," the boy mumbled.

There were a few loud guffaws at the funny name, and the boy glanced about, scowling again.

"Quiet, please," Caroline said, giving her sternest look. "I will have order in the classroom or you shall all stay in during morning recess."

The room went silent immediately. Caroline turned back to John. "Now, John Friday, generally I would need to have you stay inside during recess because you are tardy, but I will be lenient on you today if you promise to be on time tomorrow and from here after."

"Yes, ma'am, I promise," John whispered. "I did not mean to be late."

"How old are you, John?" Caroline asked.

"Eight," the boy said.

"And what reader did you use last year?"

"Didn't," the boy mumbled.

"Did you need to borrow one from your teacher?"

"No'm," the boy said, and then whispered something.

Caroline leaned forward. "I am sorry, I did not understand what you said. Please speak up."

"I never came to school before," the boy said.

A rustling rose up from the boys' side of the room, but there was no laughter.

"All right, then," Caroline said. "Why don't you sit in the third row for now with the other boys your age, and once we have started our lessons, we'll see where you belong."

John glanced to the third row, where three boys sat, and back to Caroline again. He still looked as though he might rush out the door, but Caroline nodded and he quietly took his seat.

"Now I shall continue taking roll," Caroline told the room. Besides John, there was one new boy and a new girl. When all the names and ages were written, Caroline closed the book and put it away.

"First lesson," she announced. "We shall begin with reading and writing."

Caroline set about dividing the room into classes. The oldest girls were all in one class, the Fourth Reader, and Eliza's friends were in another, the Third. Both classes could work by themselves once she gave them their lesson. She assigned them each a passage from their readers to copy into their copy-books. She would have them stand one by one and read the passages out loud once they were finished, and she would mark their penmanship and spelling.

Once the older classes were working quietly, Caroline went down through the rows. There were a handful of boys and girls in the Second Reader class, and only one little girl, named Ellie Simms, in the First Reader. Caroline decided to have the Second Readers recite the ABCs backward and forward, as Mr. Linney had always done, before they began their copying. As she walked between the desks, listening to the voices, she soon realized that John was mumbling. He wasn't really saying the ABCs at all.

"John, I would like you to stand and recite the ABCs by yourself," she announced.

"Can't," he mumbled.

The boys closest to him nudged one another but kept quiet.

Everyone watched to see what would happen next. Caroline knew they all expected her to rap John's knuckles with a ruler for being disobedient. Mr. Linney, who had been lenient in many ways, had always used the ruler when a scholar was lazy or did not mind him.

"Second Reader, please copy the paragraph on page one," Caroline said. "And Ellie, please sit quietly until I can work with you." She turned and went back to her desk and beckoned for John to follow. "Now, John, please tell me why you can't say your ABCs."

"Because I don't know 'em," whispered John, looking down at the floor.

"Oh!" Caroline said, realizing she had

made a mistake. She should have asked John if he knew how to read and write instead of assuming that since he was all of eight years old, his folks had taught him something even if he had not been to school before.

"I am sorry, John," Caroline continued. "I should have asked you if you knew your alphabet."

John seemed surprised that the teacher would be apologizing to him. "Aw, that's all right, he said. "I want to learn to read and write. That's why I came here."

"Of course, John!" Caroline said enthusiastically. "And I will teach you." She knew John would feel awkward being in a class with Ellie, a little girl half his age, because the older boys might make fun of him. But there was no way around it.

"You and Ellie will make up my First Reader class," Caroline said, and then she leaned in close. "You seem like a bright boy, and I'm sure you'll pick things up in no time. Then you can help Ellie if she has trouble. How does that sound?"

John gave a small smile and nodded approvingly.

"Good, then!" Caroline said. She hurried to check on the Second Readers to see how they were progressing, and then she brought Ellie and John up front so she could work with them at her desk. Ellie had her own reader and slate and piece of chalk, but John had nothing. Caroline took out one of the extra slates and pieces of chalk from her desk, and brought out her old reader.

"You may use these during the day while you are at school," she said.

"I can?" John asked, staring down at the items in awe.

"Yes, you may," Caroline automatically corrected.

"Th-thank you, ma'am," John stammered.

For a quarter of an hour Caroline worked with her First Reader class. Ellie was only four and easily distracted, but John worked diligently on copying his letters.

When she was dismissing them, she made sure to praise both, but it was to John she gave special words of encouragement.

"Very good, John," Caroline said. "I think you'll pick this up in short order."

"Thank you, Miss Quiner!" he murmured, looking down at what he had copied so far on his slate.

Now Caroline turned her attention to the older classes again. She listened to their recitations and graded their copybooks. When she glanced at the clock, she was surprised to see that it was already time for recess. The morning was going by very quickly.

She brought the room to order and dismissed them all. The boys and young girls scrambled for the door right away, to get the most out of their fifteen minutes of play.

John did not go outside with the others. He asked if he could have a drink of water, and then he asked if he could sit at his desk and continue copying his ABCs onto his slate.

"Yes, you may, John," Caroline answered.

Eliza came to get a drink of water from the tin cup, and then she stopped and whispered in Caroline's ear, "You are doing so well!"

"Thank you!" Caroline whispered back, smiling. It did seem that things were going well. She did not feel nervous anymore. She was busy and confident. Her hands weren't trembling and her insides were calm.

After morning recess it was time for geography and history. Polly's class began studying the countries of Europe, their capitals, and their kings and queens.

"Why don't we have a queen like they do in some of those other countries?" little Tobias Gentry asked when Caroline moved on to work with the younger classes on the history and geography of their own American states.

"We don't believe in kings or queens here in this country," Caroline replied. "We elect our presidents because we are a democracy. We do have a first lady, however. She is the wife of the president, and she entertains guests of the White House and stands by her husband's side as he leads our country."

Tobias's hand shot up in the air again. "But President Buchanan don't have no wife!" he said when Caroline called on him.

"President Buchanan does not have a wife," Caroline corrected, smiling. "You are right, Tobias! President Buchanan is a bachelor, our only president thus far who has been unmarried. His niece, Miss Harriet Lane, acts as our first lady."

For another half hour Caroline listened while the younger scholars recited the names of the presidents and the states and their capitals. She was surprised that John could answer many of the questions she posed to the class. He knew a little history and geography even if he did not yet know how to read or write.

When it was nearly noon, Caroline told the scholars to close their books. "You are dismissed for dinner," she said.

Again there was a rush for the door. The boys and girls who lived in town would go home for dinner, and the rest would eat from the pails they had brought and play in the school yard until it was time for lessons again.

Caroline noticed that John was slow to get up from his desk.

A Good First Day

"Can I stay in here and study, Miss Quiner?" he asked.

"May I," Caroline corrected.

"May I stay, Miss Quiner?"

Caroline hesitated. "It's such a nice day, John—why don't you run outside and play with the other boys?"

John glanced at the door and back at the reader Caroline had lent him.

"Yes, ma'am," John said reluctantly, setting the book down on his desk and turning for the door.

Eliza brought the dinner pail Caroline had packed that morning and set it on the teacher's desk.

"I'll stay and eat with you if you like," Eliza said, but Caroline could tell that she really wanted to go outside with her friends.

"Don't be silly," Caroline said, smiling. "I'll just take my half, and you can go with Margaret and Mary."

As Eliza was leaving, Polly and Maddy and the other older girls approached with their dinner pails. Maddy always used to go home

47

to the store to eat with her folks. But last term she had begun to stay, saying that she preferred sitting and chatting with her friends during dinnertime.

"May we join you?" Polly asked now.

"Yes, please do!" Caroline said. She had already decided that it would be fine to sit with her friends while she ate. If she had work to do, or if she had to stay in with a scholar, then she would do so.

"How do you like being our schoolteacher, Miss Quiner?" Maddy asked right away, an eyebrow archly raised.

"I like it very much!" Caroline replied.

"Well, I know I wouldn't like it at all!" Maddy announced. "Too much work organizing all the different classes and keeping all the scholars in order!"

Caroline exchanged an amused smile with Polly. Maddy had always been that way—quick to speak her mind. And she was an only child to boot. She had never had to manage a younger sibling, and so she wasn't used to it.

"I would be terribly nervous to teach school

all by myself, but you seem cool as a cucumber," Polly said then.

"Well, I was a little nervous at first," Caroline admitted.

"Were you?" Polly asked in surprise. "It didn't show at all."

After they had eaten dinner, Polly brought out her sewing and Maddy and Elmira took out the mufflers they were knitting. The girls settled in to chat about Concord news. Polly and her sister Lydia had just visited Nell, so Polly told all about Nell's little house and about the handsome baby boy.

"Nell chose her husband wisely, I think," Maddy said importantly. "Jacob is planning on a big crop of wheat, that's for certain. He bought a heap of seed from my father."

Maddy knew a great deal about the goings-on in town because men were always stopping in her father's store to do business or just to chat.

"I heard that Mr. Linney bought a piece of land from Mr. Kellogg," Maddy continued.

"I can't see Mr. Linney as a farmer, can

you?" Polly asked Caroline.

Caroline shook her head. She had respected Mr. Linney because he had been a dedicated schoolmaster, but she recalled how he had had the most delicate hands of any man she had ever seen. She could not really imagine him farming. She wondered that he did not return east with his inheritance. He had spoken often of missing Boston.

"I suppose he'll be looking for a wife now that he has money and property," Maddy said, and then she let out a laugh. "Oh, can you imagine marrying Skinny Linney?"

The girls burst into giggles, but Caroline kept quiet. The idea of marrying Mr. Linney was amusing, but it would never do to have the teacher laughing over gossip.

Polly must have sensed what Caroline was feeling. She became serious before the others, and then she said, "Well, girls, now that dinner is through, why don't we take a turn around the schoolhouse before recess is over? I for one would like a bit of fresh air to clear my head before afternoon lessons."

"Yes, that would be nice," Maddy agreed.

As the girls packed up their pails and their knitting and sewing, Caroline gave Polly a grateful look. She was happy to have some time to herself before afternoon lessons began.

After her friends had gone outside, Caroline cleaned the blackboard again and planned her lessons for the afternoon. "What must be done is best done quickly," Mother always said. Caroline had never liked arithmetic nearly as much as she liked grammar and spelling. She decided to get the dreaded subject out of the way so that the rest of the afternoon could be spent on something she found pleasing.

When it was nearly one o'clock, Caroline walked outside with her handbell and glanced about the school yard. All the scholars who had gone into town for dinner had returned. The boys were playing a game of snap-the-whip while the girls sat or stood in little groups in the shade of the schoolhouse. John was off by himself, drawing with a stick in the dirt. Caroline gave a little inward sigh. She hoped John would make friends soon.

Caroline rang the bell, and the scholars all filed inside for afternoon lessons.

"We shall begin with arithmetic," Caroline announced once everyone was settled. She heard a few disappointed sighs, and inwardly she sympathized with them. "Please take out your books if you have them."

For an hour Caroline did her best to make adding and subtracting and dividing and multiplying seem exciting. For the older class, all she could do was copy problems on the board and give her friends assistance working through the problems if they needed it. But for the Second and Third Reader classes, who were studying multiplication, she decided to make a little game by having the girls and boys compete against one another, running through their tables as if it were a spelldown.

The game worked very well. The room was full of bright, interested eyes, which was not usually the case directly after dinnertime. Even the scholars who weren't participating in the game—the older girls and little Ellie and John—were intently watching and waiting to see who would remain standing.

To Caroline's surprise, it was Docia Ingalls who won. She could rattle off all the multiplication tables without batting an eye. Caroline praised Docia and wrote her name in a special place at the top corner of the blackboard.

"You are our champion today, Docia," Caroline said. "Once a week we shall have the same game, and we'll see if you have any challenges to your victory."

Caroline noticed determined looks on many young faces. She had given them a challenge, and now the scholars would work harder at learning their multiplication tables. Caroline remembered how Miss May had used games to "stimulate learning," as she had said. She believed that children could be taught to love learning, rather than dread it, and Caroline agreed.

The last two hours, spent on grammar and spelling, went so quickly that Caroline could hardly believe it when she glanced up at the clock and saw that it was four o'clock already. She told the scholars to close their books and straighten their desks, then dismissed them for the day.

"Are you worn out from your first day as teacher?" Eliza asked, once the schoolroom was empty and she was helping Caroline tidy up.

Caroline shook her head. She was *tired*, but not worn out. The bigger boys had all behaved themselves after their initial outburst over John Friday, and the girls had been sweet as lambs.

"It was a good first day," Caroline said, glad to her very bones.

Gifts

The second day went as smoothly as the first. A week of teaching flew by, and over the quiet weekend Caroline found that she could hardly wait for Monday morning to come again.

"It sounds like torture to me," Martha said on Sunday, after Caroline had told her about some of the things that had happened at school. "Why do you like it so much?"

"I like teaching because it's something new and different every day," Caroline said. "Each day comes with its own challenge."

"What do you mean? Don't you do the same old lessons every day just like Skinny—I mean *Mr.* Linney—used to do?" Martha caught Caroline's eye and slyly smiled.

"But even when you do the same lessons, there are surprises," Caroline answered. "Like on Friday, when little Ruby Sharpe was talking and passing notes during arithmetic. I was really surprised, because she had been quiet and mindful up until then. Once I sat her down and talked with her, I realized that actually the problem had to do with her not liking arithmetic. She hadn't learned her lesson because she didn't understand it. So I told her how I never liked arithmetic either, and that we would work together. That solved everything."

"Well, it was only the first week," Martha said skeptically. "You might not feel the same way after another. And little Ruby Sharpe may give you trouble again, since you were easy on her and didn't punish her. Wait and see."

Caroline hoped Martha was wrong. All that

week she kept the scholars on their toes with word games and multiplying competitions and spelldowns. The lessons were always lively, and the scholars all seemed willing and able. She didn't have to punish anyone.

Ruby Sharpe did not whisper or pass notes once during arithmetic. Caroline was pleased, and when she came to help the girl with an especially difficult problem, Ruby's huge grin as she suddenly understood was like a gift.

Caroline had never felt so needed. She knew that was why she liked teaching so much. She wanted to tell Martha, but she didn't think her older sister would understand. Martha would say that of course Caroline had always been needed. There had always been so much to do around the house and farm. Mother had always needed Caroline to do her share.

Somehow, being needed at home was not the same as being needed at school. At home Martha or Eliza could always step in to feed the chickens and geese or do the washing and baking or help with the garden.

At school there was only one teacher. The young scholars wholly relied on Caroline to teach them what they didn't know, and the older girls needed Caroline to guide them through their studies.

As the weeks passed, Caroline grew more and more attuned to individual needs and abilities. Docia was good at arithmetic but not at spelling, so Caroline urged her to work harder at studying her speller. Ruby Sharpe was a whip at spelling, but she still needed extra encouragement with her long division. Caroline's own sister Eliza had perfect penmanship, but she was not so good at recitations, and Caroline had to gently chide her into working harder on her memorization.

It was important to praise her scholars' strengths, Caroline felt, while helping them with any weaknesses. She shuddered when she recalled the many teachers she had had over the years who seemed to delight in tormenting children by pointing out their mistakes. She remembered one teacher in particular who had actually mimicked his scholars when they mispronounced a word.

Caroline wanted the scholars to learn for learning's sake, and it thrilled her when a boy or girl really understood something he or she had been struggling with. Caroline was especially pleased with John Friday's progress.

In a very short time John had mastered the alphabet and was able to read and write simple words and sentences. She was amazed at his diligence and perseverance.

Caroline had told Eliza that she would have no favorites, but she found herself paying special attention to the boy. Often she sat with him during recess so that she could help him catch up with the other children his age.

She began to notice that John brought very little food with him for his dinner. Sometimes he had a hard roll with some pork fat tucked into his coat pocket, but more often than not he had nothing at all. He was very thin and small as it was. On the days he had no dinner, he was listless and distracted in the afternoons, unable to concentrate well on his lessons.

Caroline understood his hunger all too well.

She recalled vividly the lean years right after her father's death. How poor they had been! Often Caroline had spent the whole day with a painfully empty stomach because Mother could feed them only a little cornmeal and water—Mother's mush, they used to call it.

So she began packing a little extra in her dinner pail to offer John. She knew he would not take the food outright. He was a proud little boy. On the days they worked together, Caroline would eat a little and then say something like "Goodness, I cannot eat another bite of this. Would you help me finish it?"

At first John would shake his head and reply that he was not hungry. Gradually, though, he began to glance at the food and say, "Well, if you're not going to eat it, I hate to see good food go to waste."

Caroline was happy to help in what small way she could, but she wondered about his family. He still came to school looking like a ragamuffin. What kind of mother would not take the time to patch the holes in her son's britches?

One day Caroline decided that as the schoolteacher, she had a duty to find out something about his home life.

"John, you are doing so well now, I would like to tell your mother and father about your progress," Caroline said as they were sitting together going over his spelling for the day. "I would like to pay your parents a visit. Where do you live?"

John's eyes lit up for a moment at the compliment, but quickly dimmed.

"Pa's not home much," John said. "He works at the inn mostly."

"For Mr. Kellogg?" Caroline asked in surprise. Mr. Larrimore managed the inn, and she had never heard of a Mr. Friday.

"Yes, ma'am," he replied.

"Well, then I'll pay a visit to your mother," Caroline said.

"Ain't got none," he mumbled, looking down at his lap.

"Oh," Caroline said quietly. She did not correct his *ain't* as she normally would have. "I am sorry, John," she said instead. "I know what it's like to lose a parent. My father passed away when I was five years old."

John glanced up at her, eyes full of surprise, then back down again. "Ma went when I was four." He began to play with a button on his sleeve that was about to come off and added quietly, "Sometimes I don't remember her so good even though I want to."

Caroline nodded. She knew exactly how he felt. She tried to think of something good and helpful to say, and then she remembered words Mother had used once long ago when Caroline had worried about forgetting Father.

"Memories fade over time, but your mother is always here in your heart." She reached out and tapped gently on John's chest. "Your mother will always be with you, John. And I know she would be very proud of how hard you are working here at school."

The boy sniffed and wiped his nose on his sleeve. Caroline reached into her desk drawer for a clean handkerchief.

"You may take this and return it to me at another time," Caroline said.

John nodded. He used the handkerchief and tucked it carefully in his pocket.

"I think you've finished this lesson now, John," Caroline said softly. "I'm very pleased with your work today. Why don't you go outside to get some fresh air before I ring the bell."

"Yes, Miss Quiner," John answered, getting up from his seat. At the door, he stopped and turned. "Miss Quiner, why do you spend so much time with me?"

"Because you are bright, John, and because you are willing to learn," Caroline said.

John took a deep breath and said in a rush, "You must be the best teacher in the whole world!" Then he turned and ran out the door.

Again Caroline felt she had been given a gift, a gift of pure gold.

That night while she was alone in the kitchen with Mother after supper, Caroline told her a little about John and how happy she felt to be able to teach him to read and write.

"I must say teaching agrees with you, Caroline," Mother said. "You look so lively these days. Your eyes are bright and your cheeks are full of color."

"Why, Mother!" Caroline laughed, but she didn't know what else to say.

Alone in the girls' room before bed, she stared at herself in the mirror. She had always thought her nose was too long and her mouth too wide, but she did look different somehow. Perhaps it was because she *felt* different. She had never before felt so confident and sure of herself.

Independence Day

The days grew longer, and spring abruptly gave way to summer. June had blown in hot and dry, and July promised to be even hotter.

"Goodness, I can't recall a hotter Fourth, can you?" Martha sighed as Caroline tugged at her corset strings.

It was the glorious Fourth of July—Independence Day. There was no school, of course. Caroline and her sisters had already done the household chores, and now they were putting on their Sunday best for the celebrations in town.

The celebrations were small compared to Brookfield's, but there was a speech and usually some music and lemonade, and it was a chance to visit with friends and neighbors. Caroline had already helped pack a picnic basket of roast chicken, biscuits, potatoes, cucumber pickles, and two kinds of pie—blueberry and strawberry.

"I wish I didn't have to wear this corset when it's so hot!" Martha said breathlessly as Caroline gave another tug.

"A lady must always wear her corset," Eliza said, repeating what Mother had always told them. "I would never go without my corset, especially on a day like today. Would you, Caroline?"

Caroline shook her head. A corset wasn't pleasant, but it was part of being grown up. When she had been at school in Milwaukee, the founder of the college, Miss Catharine Beecher, had not approved of corsets. Caroline had actually gone to a class of calisthenics

where the girls removed their corsets and danced about in loose-fitting gowns. Caroline had felt terribly awkward at first, but later she had enjoyed the class. Still, she believed as Mother did, that ladies should wear corsets every day. She knew that sometimes Martha went without hers during the week.

"When one wears a corset every day, it doesn't seem like such a chore," Caroline said pointedly, tightening the last stay.

"Oh, that's tight enough!" Martha exclaimed breathlessly. "It doesn't matter anyway. My waist has never been as slim as yours, Caroline, and it never will be."

"Let's compare," Eliza said, taking a tape measure from her sewing basket. "Caroline does win the prize. Her waist matches her age exactly—seventeen and a half inches."

"Well, Charlie likes me just as I am!" Martha said, chin in the air. She turned to finish dressing. Caroline and Eliza exchanged an amused glance and did the same.

Caroline had chosen to wear the blue-and-white-checked silk from the dressmaker in Milwaukee. The smooth fabric felt mercifully cool against her skin, and the scooping neckline was not as confining as a high-necked collar would be. The blue of the checks matched her eyes exactly.

Martha wore the deep-blue calico she had made herself with a pattern copied from *Godey's Lady's Book*. It had a scooped neckline, wide sleeves, and a bell skirt, just like Caroline's.

Eliza's good dress was a yellow poplin that had been Caroline's. Mother had fashionably reworked the dress with wider, lacy sleeves and a lacy flounce at the bottom.

"I'm the only one in hand-me-downs today." Eliza sighed as the girls stood all together at the mirror.

"That dress never looked that good on me, truly, Eliza," Caroline said cheerfully, wanting to make her sister feel better. Until she'd gone away to college, Caroline had always had to wear Martha's old dresses and shoes, so she knew how Eliza felt.

Just then the girls heard the jingle of a

harness, and they hurried to the window. A shiny black buggy came rolling out of the woods. It circled the clearing, a familiar bay pony trotting jauntily in front.

"It's Charlie!" Eliza exclaimed. "And he's driving a new buggy! Oh, Martha, I guess you'll be going to town in style!"

The buggy was very fashionable. It was small—only big enough for two, with a cushioned leather seat and a bonnet that had been rolled back and tied.

Charlie tugged on the reins, and the horse and buggy stopped just below the girls' window. He swept his hat from his head and grinned up at them. He had always been a handsome boy, and now he was a handsome young man. His thick black hair had been smoothed down with bear grease, and his beard was trim and neat.

Eliza began to giggle and wave at Charlie, but Martha grew suddenly sober. Her cheeks flushed pink and she turned back to the mirror.

"Oh, do you think I look all right?" she

asked, fussing with her bodice and sounding much less sure of herself than she had before.

"You look beautiful, Martha," Caroline said truthfully. She came to stand beside her sister at the mirror. "That dress is perfect on you."

"Do you really think so?" Martha asked.

"Yes," Caroline said. "Charlie will be proud to have you at his side today."

For as long as Caroline could remember, Charlie had had this same effect on Martha. Even when they were children, growing up together in Brookfield, Martha had been in awe of him. Martha, who could be fierce as a lion, was more like a lamb around Charlie. It was love, Caroline supposed, that made Martha change so completely. Caroline had never been in love, but she did not think it would make *her* into such a wholly different person.

The girls tied on their bonnets, pulled on their gloves, and hurried downstairs. Pa and Thomas and Mother and Lottie were outside, all gathered around Charlie. Mother was asking after Charlie's folks, who were old friends of theirs, but Thomas was more interested in the new buggy.

"How fast does it go?" he asked as soon as Charlie had answered all Mother's questions.

"Fast as the wind," Charlie boasted. "It's light as a feather, so the horse doesn't even know we're there!"

"Hey, maybe we could race it against some fellows in town!" Thomas proposed.

"Well, now, your sister gets the first ride," Charlie replied with a wink. He looked at Martha and grinned. "What do you think, *Miss* Martha? Does this buggy suit you?" he asked.

Martha blushed deeply. Charlie had teased her with "Miss Martha" as a girl, and it always made her smile. "It's a fine buggy, Charlie," she said.

"If you're ready, we'd best hurry along. We don't want to miss anything in town, and I want to show you how smooth this buggy rides," Charlie said.

"Do be careful, Charlie," Mother spoke up then. "I want my daughter home all in one piece."

"Why, of course, Mrs. Holbrook, I'll take good care of Miss Martha," Charlie promised.

"Oh, I wish I had a handsome suitor with a new buggy," Eliza whispered as Martha and Charlie waved and disappeared into the woods.

"Well, we'd best hurry along, too, I reckon," Pa said, his brown eyes sparkling down at Mother. "Charlie Carpenter's not the only one with pretty ladies to escort to town."

"Why, thank you, Frederick," Mother said, laughing.

It was Lottie's first time going to town for Independence Day, and she was so excited she could hardly speak. She held tightly to Caroline's hand as they sat together in the back of Pa's wagon, rolling toward Territorial Road. Already they could hear the *pop! pop! pop!* of firecrackers coming through the trees, and with each *pop!* Lottie's eyes seemed to grow bigger.

When they reached Territorial Road, it was crowded with other wagons and horses and families on foot. Everyone dressed in their Sunday best.

"Good day to you!"

"A fine day for a celebration!"

"Happy Independence Day!"

The greetings rang out all around, and boys darted through the crowd, lighting firecrackers and throwing them into the air.

Pop! pop! pop!

Lottie let out a little squeal and jumped up and down in her seat when one of the firecrackers came close.

"Hold still," Caroline admonished, but not very forcefully. Seeing Lottie this excited made Caroline smile. She vividly recalled celebrations in Brookfield when she was a little girl. How she had loved marching in the parades and singing the patriotic tunes! It was the one day of the year she had longed to be a boy, so that she could shout out her pride to be an American at the top of her lungs.

"Hey, there's Henry and Joseph!" Thomas said, interrupting Caroline's thoughts. The brothers were farther up the road, but as Thomas called out to them, they turned and waited for the wagon.

Independence Day

Caroline saw them so rarely that it was always something of a shock to realize that Joseph and Henry were men now, not boys. Both were handsome in the dark Sunday suits Mother had made them last year, and even if they were on the lean side—hungry, as Eliza had said—they looked strong and capable and confident.

"Happy Fourth!" Joseph called when they had caught up. "We were keeping an eye out for you all!"

Joseph and Henry hopped up onto the wagon bed as it rolled along.

Henry grinned at Caroline. "How's the schoolteacher these days?"

"Fine and dandy, thank you very much," Caroline replied.

"Are any of those boys giving you trouble at your school?" Joseph asked.

"Not a bit." Caroline shook her head. "They're only small boys."

"Well, we'll ask you again in the winter, when you have the bigger boys to contend with." Henry glanced around. "Hey, where's Martha?"

"Charlie came for her in a new buggy!" Thomas announced.

Henry let out a low whistle. "That boy must be pretty confident about his wheat crop."

In town, horses and buggies were tied all down the length of Main Street. Crowds of people milled about. It took some time for Pa to drive the wagon through all the hubbub. At Mr. Kellogg's inn a group of men was standing together on the porch, and the American flag flew from the tall flagpole out front. The red, white, and blue was glorious against the bright, brilliant blue of the sky, and Caroline felt gooseflesh rise on her arms.

"Look, Lottie," Caroline said, pointing. "See the flag?"

Lottie nodded wordlessly, staring up.

"Today is so much fun, with all the firecrackers and music and crowds, but all the celebrating we do is in honor of that flag," Caroline continued. "And one of those pretty white stars stands for our own state of

Wisconsin. On Independence Day we make all this noise in honor of the battles the first Americans fought so that all of us could be free. Do you understand, Lottie?"

Lottie nodded solemnly, turning to keep her eyes on the flag as they passed by.

"Spoken just like a teacher," Henry joked.

"And very well put," Mother said over her shoulder.

Henry grinned his familiar wide, toothy grin at Caroline—the donkey grin, Caroline had called it when they were young. It had always made her laugh. "I guess I sound like a teacher because I am one!" she said, nudging Henry playfully.

"Well!" Henry said. "I hope you're not getting too big for your britches. You're still Little Brownbraid to me."

"Little Brownbraid?" Lottie asked. "But you don't wear your hair in a braid! You wear it up like a lady."

"That was my nickname when I was as small as you," Caroline said, tugging gently on one of Lottie's curls.

It suddenly seemed impossible to Caroline that she had ever been as young as Lottie. So much time had passed—fifteen years since her own father had first called her Little Brownbraid. Caroline still thought of her father often and missed him, though she had grown to love her new pa.

The wagon turned into the school yard, where the picnicking would be. Already the clearing was filled with friends and neighbors.

"Shall I unpack the baskets now, Mother?" Caroline asked after Henry had helped her down from the wagon.

"No, why don't you mingle a little," Mother replied. "I'll stay here and get things ready."

"Don't you want us to stay with you?" Caroline asked.

"No, no!" Mother answered. "I see Mrs. Scott and Mrs. Rhodes over yonder. I'll do some visiting while you all see what's happening on Main Street."

"I want to get some firecrackers!" Thomas announced.

Independence Day

Pa reached into his pocket and gave Thomas a nickel. "Don't spend it all on puffs of smoke and noise!" Pa said, but Thomas was already headed off, with Joseph and Henry following behind him.

"We'll keep him out of trouble," Henry called over his shoulder, but Caroline doubted Henry's ability to keep anybody, including himself, out of mischief.

Pa tethered the oxen to a stake, then went off to see what the men were discussing on Mr. Kellogg's porch. Caroline and Eliza took Lottie between them and strolled back toward Main Street.

"So many people!" Lottie whispered.

Caroline nodded. It was a lot of people for Concord, but of course it couldn't compare to the crowds she had seen in Milwaukee.

"Hello, Miss Quiner!" a group of little girls from school called as they passed.

"Hello, girls," Caroline answered.

Next a group of young boys dashed by, chasing after a pig that had gotten loose from somewhere. "Hullo, Miss Quiner!" they shouted as they ran. "Happy Fourth!"

"Do *we* have to call you Miss Quiner today?" a voice asked. It was Polly, an amused expression on her pretty face. Maddy was with her.

"Of course not!" Caroline laughed.

"Oh, you look so stylish in that dress, Caroline!" Polly gushed. "I declare you are the best-dressed girl in Concord."

Caroline noticed Maddy's lips turn down in a quick frown. Maddy had so many pretty dresses, Caroline knew she probably considered herself to be the best dressed.

"Thank you for the compliment," Caroline politely said. "But I think you two look splendid. That lavender is very becoming on you, Maddy."

Maddy clasped one of Caroline's hands and said, "I do so love these little lace gloves you brought back from the city. I've asked my father to order some for the store."

"Oh, I can't wait!" Polly exclaimed. "Now shall we all take a stroll together?"

"Yes, let's do!" Caroline said, turning to see

what had become of Eliza and Lottie.

Eliza had found Margaret and Mary, and the girls wanted to keep Lottie with them, so Caroline was free to stroll with her friends. Together they went slowly up the length of Main Street and back down again. Young men tipped their hats to the girls as they passed. Several buggies rushed by with couples in them, stirring up dust. Martha and Charlie went rolling by at a fast clip, and Caroline waved to them.

"They are a handsome couple," Polly commented.

Suddenly Mr. Linney came up beside the girls, riding a fine black horse. He looked much tidier than he ever had as schoolmaster. Instead of the faded baggy black suit he habitually wore when teaching, he now sported a crisp gray jacket and trousers that fit his thin frame perfectly.

"Good morning, young ladies," he said brightly, tipping a black felt hat. "I trust you are enjoying yourselves on this wonderful day?"

"Oh, yes, thank you, Mr. Linney," Maddy spoke up.

"Well, good!" Mr. Linney said. He seemed to want to say more, but then he nervously tipped his hat again. "Good day to you all!"

"Good day!" the girls said together.

After he had moved away, Caroline waited for Maddy to giggle or say something amusing about Mr. Linney's startling change in appearance, but she kept strangely quiet, watching the horse and rider as they trotted down the street.

Caroline turned to Polly. "Where are your folks today?"

"Pa and the boys are around here some-where, and Lydia and Docia are visiting Nell," Polly said. "Ma stayed home. She thought it would be too much for Ruby and baby Lansford."

When the girls neared the inn, they found a small crowd had gathered.

"Lemonade! Come and get your nice fresh lemonade! It's free for all on this fourth day of

July!" Mr. Larrimore shouted.

Four large barrels had been lined up in front of the porch, and Mr. Larrimore and his wife were filling tin cups and passing them out. Eliza and Margaret and Lottie were already waiting in line for their turn, and so were Joseph and his friends.

"Let's hurry and get a drink before they get to the bottom of the barrel and the lemonade's warm!" Maddy said.

When Mrs. Larrimore finally handed Caroline one of the tin cups, the lemonade was tangy and sweet and wonderfully cold. Caroline savored the treat as long as she could. She had just handed the cup back to Mrs. Larrimore with her thanks when she heard a voice call out, "Hey, save some for us!"

Caroline turned to see Henry and another young man making their way through the crowd. The young man wore a straw hat with a wide brim that covered his face, and for a moment Caroline did not think she knew him. But then he pushed back the brim to reveal a familiar face.

"Charles Ingalls! Why, you're a stranger in these parts!" Joseph cried, slapping the newcomer on the back.

"Came home for the celebrations, did you, Charles?" asked Jonah Crab.

Caroline watched as the young men greeted one another and shook hands. Charles Ingalls was one of Polly's older brothers. Caroline supposed it had been nearly two years since she had last seen him—and he had been called "Charlie" back then.

Like Henry and Joseph, Charles had grown up in that time. He was taller and broader about the shoulders. His face was brown from the sun, and he looked handsome in his good black suit. The more formal name of Charles suited him now, Caroline decided.

"Good afternoon, Polly," Charles said in mock formality, giving his sister a little bow and removing his hat. His thick brown hair was slicked back like that of the other young men. He turned to Maddy and Caroline and bowed again. "Good afternoon, ladies."

"How nice to see you back home, Charles," Maddy said. "Did your brother come with you?"

"No, Peter couldn't be persuaded to leave his land," Charles said. "But I wasn't going to stay away from company on such a fine occasion as this. It's nice to join together and celebrate being free and independent, don't you think?"

Charles turned to Caroline and raised an eyebrow as he spoke, so that it seemed he was posing the question just to her.

"Yes, I do!" Caroline responded enthusiastically. "It is the most important holiday for us as Americans, and we should certainly be proud to honor the sacrifices our forefathers made."

"Yes, Miss Quiner," Henry joked, "but school's out today, didn't you know?"

Caroline knew the color was rising in her cheeks. She had not meant to sound so formal. She had only wanted to agree with Charles, and she did feel strongly about Independence Day. She had spent the whole week during history lessons reading about redcoats and Paul Revere and how men just like their own brothers and fathers had beaten down the trained British Army. All the scholars had worked hard on memorizing the Declaration of Independence, and had done their recitations splendidly.

But she did feel silly for speaking so forcefully, and so she decided to make light of the moment. She gave Henry a nudge with her elbow, and said, "Well, Henry, I would certainly have my hands full if you were still in school. I'm afraid I'd have to resort to the switch to keep you in line."

"School's out for good for me, Miss Quiner!" Henry said, pretending to ward off a switching.

They all laughed, and so did Caroline.

"I agree with the teacher, and so should you all!" Charles cried. "It *is* our most important holiday! Being free is something worth celebrating, and celebrating well!"

"Hear, hear!" Henry called, saluting.

Caroline glanced at Charles and was surprised to find him watching her. For some reason she felt herself blushing again, and she politely smiled and looked away. It was strange, but she wasn't sure, in all the time she had known Charles, she had ever realized how very blue his eyes were.

"Anyway, I am ready to celebrate now! Let's get us some of that lemonade!" Henry said, tugging at Charles's arm.

Charles let himself be led away, but he turned and tipped his hat to the girls as he went.

In a little while Caroline heard the sound of lively music. It was Mr. Fleming on the fife and Mr. Biles on the drum, playing "The Star-Spangled Banner." A line of children had formed behind them, clapping and singing as they began to march down Main Street. Lottie had joined the little parade, and she waved at Caroline as she passed.

When Henry and Charles joined the girls again, Polly cocked her head and playfully asked, "Did you two save some lemonade for the rest of the town?"

"Well, I tried to drink one whole barrel,

but Mrs. Larrimore stopped me," Henry answered, winking. "I tell you, I could drink the whole lot and still be thirsty, it's that hot!"

"If it's this hot in July, I hate to see what August will be," Charles agreed, shaking his head.

"You and Peter have a wheat crop this year?" Henry asked.

Charles nodded. "As long as we get rain, we'll be fine."

The parade wound its way back down Main Street, coming close again, and a crowd of people surged forward to watch the children. Caroline found herself separated from Polly and Maddy and Henry, but Charles was still at her side when the parade snaked away and the crowd dispersed.

"So you are farming up north now, Charles?" she asked.

Charles nodded. "It's my brother Peter's land, but I'm helping him clear it. That's why I haven't been back here much. We've been working all year on it." He squinted off into the distance and back at Caroline again. "You were away some too, weren't you? You went off to Milwaukee for a time?"

"Yes, I was attending college," Caroline answered.

"That must have been something," Charles said, and Caroline nodded. "You liked the big city, then? Lots to do there, I reckon."

"Oh yes, there were always theatricals and music recitals and meetings to attend." Caroline paused. She didn't want it to sound as if all her time was spent frivolously. "I had to do a lot of studying though. And I was so happy to come home again."

"And now you're teaching school, and doing a fine job, I hear. Apparently, Docia will talk of no one else at home but 'Miss Quiner.'"

"How sweet!" Caroline said, pleased. "Docia is a smart girl. She's a whip at her multiplication tables."

"You were always good at spelling, as I recall," Charles said. "You were always spelling everybody down, including me!"

"You were able to beat me once," Caroline said, suddenly remembering.

Charles gazed down at her and his blue eyes twinkled again. "That's right, I did beat you, but only one time!"

Just then the little parade came to a stop right in front of the inn. Mr. Fleming played a last trilling high note on his fife and Mr. Biles beat his drum in a final crescendo. The crowd burst into applause.

Lottie rushed over and twined her hand through Caroline's.

"That looked like fun," Caroline said, taking out her handkerchief and wiping some dust from Lottie's cheek. She smoothed the ribbon holding back Lottie's pretty blond curls.

"Oh yes, it was!" Lottie breathed, her eyes bright. "I like marching."

"I liked marching too, when I was your age," Charles said, giving Lottie a wink.

"So did I!" Caroline laughed.

"Attention, please!" Mr. Kellogg's deep voice rang out from the top of the porch steps.

Independence Day

"May I have your attention, please!"

A hush fell over the crowd. Mr. Kellogg always gave a speech on Independence Day, and then someone would recite the Declaration of Independence. Caroline wondered if there would also be music.

"Now then, good people of Concord," Mr. Kellogg began. "It is my duty and honor to come before you on this day, and so I shall get right to it!"

Mr. Kellogg's speech was nearly the same every year, but it was always moving, and he was an eloquent speaker.

He told of the tyranny of Great Britain and how Americans had risen up to declare themselves free from kings. He spoke of the terrible battles waged and the triumph of the colonists over the British army.

"Hurrah! Hurrah!" rippled through the crowd.

"We stand today, seventy-some years after that battle was won, under a flag that means freedom to us all," Mr. Kellogg continued, pointing up to where the flag flew. "I am mighty proud to be an American!"

The shouts of agreement rose up all around. Mr. Kellogg waited to continue until he could be heard.

"Some doubted that this little town of Concord would amount to much, but we're here today to celebrate not only our country's success but our own. This is a fine town, and it's growing bigger every day, and each and every one of you should be proud to call yourselves Concordians!"

"Hurrah, hurrah!" the men shouted, and the ladies clapped.

Now Mr. Kellogg announced that it was time to recite the Declaration of Independence. He called on Mr. Linney to come forward to do the honors.

"Hey, he's not the schoolteacher anymore," Henry whispered to Caroline. "They ought to have asked you to get up there."

Caroline shook her head. She knew the Declaration of Independence by heart, of course. But it was one thing to stand in front of a roomful of children, and quite another to stand before a whole town.

The crowd quieted as Mr. Linney began. He had a warm, melodious voice, and Caroline was glad that he had been chosen again to recite the powerful words.

"'When in the course of human events it becomes necessary for one people to dissolve the political bonds which have connected them with another, and to assume among the powers of the earth the separate and equal station to which the laws of Nature and of Nature's God entitle them . . .'"

Mr. Linney continued with the famous text. Caroline glanced sideways at Charles. He was listening intently to the powerful words.

Mr. Linney's voice shook a little with emotion as he came to the end. "'And for the support of this Declaration, with a firm reliance on the protection of Divine Providence, we mutually pledge to each other our Lives, our Fortunes, and our sacred Honor.'"

A solemn hush fell over the townspeople, soon broken by more shouting and clapping.

A few shots were fired into the air, and at the edge of the crowd some boys lit their firecrackers and threw them high overhead.

Pop! pop! pop!

Henry suddenly picked Caroline up and whirled her around in a circle, as if they were at a dance.

"Henry! Stop!" Caroline cried, but really she didn't mind too much.

"Now for some music!" Mr. Kellogg called, beckoning to someone near Caroline. "Come on up, Charles Ingalls, and play us a tune or two!"

Caroline turned in surprise. Charles tipped his hat to her and the others and then made his way through the parting crowd. Everyone knew Charles played the fiddle, of course. He had often played at family gatherings as a boy. Still, Caroline was impressed that Mr. Kellogg had asked him to play for the whole town. She wondered if he was nervous. But he did not seem so at all as he bounded up the porch steps and found his fiddle where it had been stowed. He greeted the crowd, then rosined up the bow and launched into a song.

It was "America," a perfect choice right after the Declaration, Caroline thought. The music tumbled forth, triumphant and strong, and human voices immediately joined the fiddle's, singing:

"My country, 'tis of thee,
Sweet land of liberty,
Of thee I sing:
Land where my fathers died,
Land of the pilgrims' pride,
From every mountainside,
Let freedom ring."

When that moving song came to an end, Charles did not wait for applause but struck up another tune right away. He played "The Star-Spangled Banner" and "Hail, Columbia" and then "Uncle Sam's Farm." One boot tapped against the floorboards in time to the music while Charles's upper body dipped and bowed with the rhythm. His thick brown hair had become unruly, sticking up in tufts about his head, and his eyes were laughing.

It was clear that Charles liked playing as much as the crowd liked listening. All about, people clapped and sang and some even jigged in place. The children could not keep still at all. Lottie was marching again, arms swinging to and fro.

Caroline remembered the first time she had ever heard Charles play. She had been a girl of twelve and he had been sixteen. She and Henry had come upon Charles, all alone in the woods, playing his fiddle—playing for the birds, as Henry had joked. His playing that day had made Caroline think that the trees themselves were singing.

And now, all these years later, Charles's playing was just as beguiling.

School Ends

Back at school on Monday, Caroline was sitting with her friends during noon recess, talking over all that had happened on Independence Day, when Maddy said, "I did not know your brother could play so well, Polly. Did someone teach him?"

"No, he just picked it up here and there," Polly answered. "He can hear a tune once and play it near perfect."

"How amazing!" Maddy said. After a moment she asked, "Is he courting anyone?"

Caroline was never surprised by Maddy's

direct questions anymore. Still, she glanced at her friend, wondering if Maddy had become interested in Charles after seeing him on Saturday.

"He says he doesn't have time for such things yet," Polly replied.

"Does he plan to settle up north near Peter?" Maddy asked.

"I don't think so," said Polly. "He's going back to help Peter for the rest of the summer, but he's always talking about heading out west when he has enough money saved—to Kansas or to California maybe."

"West! West! West!" Maddy cried in exasperation. "Why do all these young men want to go west when Concord is such a nice town just as Mr. Kellogg said?"

Caroline agreed with Maddy. She was not surprised to hear that Charles wished to go west. It seemed to her that most young men she knew yearned to travel to the western territories. Henry talked of nothing else, though he had not left as yet. Her brother's "fever" to try to strike it rich on California gold made

Caroline anxious and a little angry to boot. She just couldn't understand why anyone would want to go traipsing off to parts unknown, leaving behind family and friends, even if it meant a fortune in gold.

"I would hate to be like those women I see heading west with their husbands, their covered wagons holding all their earthly possessions, wouldn't you?" Maddy asked, turning to Caroline.

"Well, I would not like it, but my mother came all the way from Boston in a wagon. And Polly, your family moved here from New York State, didn't you?" Caroline asked.

"Yes, we did," Polly said, shrugging. "I don't mind traveling."

"I'd rather stay in one place," said Maddy firmly.

Caroline felt the same way, though she did not say so out loud. She again thought of Miss May, who had traveled here all by herself from Albany, New York. After teaching a year at Concord School, she had followed her brother to California to teach children in the mining camps there.

Caroline admired Miss May's bravery, but she herself would never want to travel so far away from home. She was happy in Concord, and she liked being useful. Being a school-teacher meant that she had a responsibility to the whole town. She wanted to help others in the same way she was helping John Friday learn to read and write.

In a way, she thought it was selfish of young men to want to go off and settle western ter-ritories when they could stay right where they were and help make their own town more prosperous. Mr. Kellogg had settled down and decided to make the town a proper place for his family. Where would Concord be with-out men like him?

All these things were whirling through Caroline's mind, and she did not pay attention to what the girls around her were saying. Then she felt a gentle nudge and heard Polly say, "Miss Quiner, a penny for your thoughts!"

Caroline glanced about her desk. All the girls were gazing at her with amused expressions.

"You were far away from us just now, Miss
Quiner," Maddy teased. "Were you mooning
over our handsome fiddler?"

"Oh, goodness, no!" Caroline cried, and her
cheeks grew warm. "I was simply mulling
over what you had said, Maddy, about all our
young men heading west. I suppose it's natural that they want to see more of this great
country of ours, but I do think the whole town
would benefit if some of them stayed put."

"There are a great many bachelors settling
here from the east, though," Elmira pointed
out. "Some of them are quite handsome!"

The girls began to compare notes on the
young men they had seen on Independence
Day. Caroline listened but kept quiet. Somehow she felt older than her friends, though
Maddy and Elmira were eighteen already.
Listening to the girls giggle over handsome
bachelors, Caroline decided that she thought
as Charles Ingalls did: She did not have time
for such things as courting yet.

And so it was with surprise that she found
her thoughts sometimes straying to Charles

during the next week. Passing Kellogg's Inn on the way to and from school, she would remember how confident and carefree Charles had seemed fiddling before the whole town, how he had instinctively known which songs to play to please the crowd.

In town Caroline kept an eye out for Charles, thinking she might come across him as he went about some errand. She wanted to tell him how very much she had enjoyed his music. At the picnic on Saturday, she had been able to speak only briefly with him, because there had always been a crowd around him after he had finished playing.

The days went by, however, and Caroline did not see Charles. When she heard from Polly that he had already returned north, she was more disappointed than she expected to be. But she did not have time to dwell on it. Summer school was coming to an end, and Caroline was so busy preparing her lessons and grading papers, she could hardly think of anything else.

She was proud of her little school. As a

whole, the classes had done exceptionally well. John Friday had excelled beyond even her best expectations, but it pained her to see how thin he was and how even more ragged his clothes had become during the term. She wondered why, if his father worked at Mr. Kellogg's inn, the boy was so poor looking. She decided to ask Maddy about it one day during noon recess.

"Mr. Friday is supposed to do odd jobs for Mr. Larrimore and some others around town, but he doesn't show up half the time," Maddy said in a confiding tone. She leaned forward and whispered, "He's a drunkard, you know. He hardly takes care of the boy at all. It really is such a shame."

"Oh, I didn't know! How terrible for John," Caroline exclaimed, her heart sinking at the news. In Milwaukee she had attended temperance meetings with her aunts. The Temperance League sought to ban liquor from being bought or sold, and also worked to give aid to families who needed it.

"It's wonderful that you take so much time

with the unfortunate boy on his lessons," Maddy said.

"I wonder how he was able to pay the money to come to school at all," Caroline mused, more to herself.

Maddy shrugged and went on to some other topic of conversation, but Caroline was lost in thought. She must do something to help John!

As soon as school was over, she went to the inn to speak with Mr. Kellogg. Surely he would know what to do to help. But Mr. Larrimore said that Mr. Kellogg had left on business that very morning, and would be gone at least a fortnight.

"Gone for so long?" Caroline murmured more to herself, wondering what she should do now.

"Anything I can help you with, Miss Quiner?" Mr. Larrimore asked kindly. "Is something wrong at the school? Perhaps you could go to another member of the school board if you're having troubles?"

"No, no, nothing is wrong at school,"

Caroline answered. She glanced about the well-furnished entryway of the inn. She had never seen Mr. Friday and wondered what he was actually like. "Does Mr. Friday work here?" she asked.

"Well, if you can call it work," Mr. Larrimore said with a look of disgust. "He's not here today in any case. And if you're wanting something fixed around the schoolhouse, I'll come myself and do it."

"No, I don't need any work done. It's just that . . ." Caroline thought for a moment and quickly decided that it was best to speak with Mr. Kellogg directly.

Walking down the street, Caroline was lost in thought. She would have to wait two weeks for Mr. Kellogg's return to see if something could be done about John's situation. In the meantime, Caroline was determined to help him herself. She would continue to bring food to school, but she also wanted to somehow get him new clothes to replace his britches and shirt, which were growing more tattered and tighter by the day.

She knew instinctively that John would never accept charity straight out, and she could not blame him. She understood how it felt to be proud and unwilling to be beholden to anybody.

In the years after Father's death, Caroline's family had been very poor. There had never been enough to eat, and shoes and clothes had been patched over and over again. Yet during all their hardship, Mother had made sure that her children were clean and decent and proud of what little they had. Mother could never abide pity or charity, and neither could Caroline.

The answer would be to help John help himself. She must think of a way of giving the boy new clothes without causing him to lose face.

That night after supper she asked Mother if she might have a set of Thomas's old clothes.

"It's for little John Friday," Caroline explained. She had often spoken of John over the past months, and so the whole family had heard of his progress and his ragged appearance. They did not know about Mr. Friday's drinking, however, and now Caroline told Mother what she had learned.

"I intend to speak with Mr. Kellogg about it when he returns from business," Caroline said. "But until then I would like to try to help him myself."

Mother's green eyes gazed intently at Caroline for a moment; then she said in a soft voice, "You were always a thoughtful child, Caroline. Let's find some clothes for that unfortunate boy!"

Mother led Caroline upstairs to the cedar chest where she kept old clothes and leftover pieces of cloth. She pulled out a pair of sturdy brown woolen trousers and two plain linen shirts she had sewn for Thomas when he was about John's age.

"These should do nicely," she said. "I would give him Thomas's old shoes if he would take them, but that may be going too far. You know, Caroline, he may not want to accept any of it."

"Yes, I know," Caroline said, biting her lip.

"Well, perhaps you could make it a prize for something he has done at school," Mother suggested.

"Yes, but I don't want to do it in front of the whole school—otherwise John would never wear the clothes. He would be too embarrassed." Caroline sighed.

"You are such a smart young lady," Mother said, gently patting Caroline's cheek. "I know you'll find a solution."

It took another day, but finally Caroline did think of something.

Each day John had been coming to school early. He helped Caroline bring in the water and sweep the floors, and often she went over some bit of homework he had found difficult the night before.

That morning when John arrived, Caroline said, "John, you do so much extra work around here, it really isn't proper!"

"It's not, ma'am?" John asked, his face clouding over with worry.

"You see, John, usually some scholar gets

into trouble and must stay and help the teacher before or after school as punishment. But all of you are so good, I haven't had to punish anyone!"

"I don't mind doing the work, Miss Quiner, honest! It's not punishment to me!" John said.

"Still, it is work, and I must repay you somehow," Caroline said. "The school cannot afford to pay you money, but I thought we could do a trade, just as some of the shopkeepers do from time to time. Would that suit you, John?"

"Why, yes, I suppose so, Miss Quiner," John answered uncertainly.

"Good!" Caroline went to her desk and brought out the clothes, neatly folded inside brown paper and tied with a string. "I am afraid it's not much, John, but this is all I can offer you in trade. It's clothes my own mother made for one of my brothers. They're quite good clothes, though, since my mother used to be a dressmaker."

"Oh, that's fine, Miss Quiner!" John said. He took the package from her, still looking uncertain.

The next day he came to school early, as usual. Caroline was grading lessons, and when she looked up, she hardly recognized him. His face was completely clean for the first time, and he had wetted and combed his hair.

Caroline was about to exclaim over how good he looked, but she caught herself in time. She did not want to embarrass him.

"Oh, John, I'm glad you've come this early!" Caroline said brightly. "I was so busy grading papers, I have not had time to sweep the entryway. Would you do that for me, after you've gotten the water?"

"Yes, Miss Quiner!" John said, quickly taking up the water pail.

While he went about his chores, Caroline noticed that he seemed more confident. She knew it must have to do with the new clothes. Outward appearances had a great impact on inward feelings, Mother had always said. When one was dirty and ragged on the outside, it was hard not to feel dirty and ragged on the inside too.

As the other scholars began to arrive,

Caroline listened for any mean comments, but none of the boys said a word, and Caroline's heart brimmed with pride to see that her little school was well-behaved.

Glancing at all the bright young faces, Caroline wished that this term would last forever. It had been very easy teaching summer school. She hoped the fall term would go as smoothly.

On the last Friday of the summer term, Caroline let the girls and boys play word and arithmetic games in the morning and then they had a spelldown in the afternoon. After that, Caroline brought out the gingerbread and lemonade she had made as a special treat.

When the little party was over, there was nothing for Caroline to do but bring the school to attention for the last time that term. She told them how well they had done, and how proud she was of each and every one of them. Then she rang the bell.

"School is dismissed for August. I hope to see you all in the fall." She felt a little forlorn as she said the words, knowing she would miss seeing these same faces staring up at her expectantly every day.

After being dismissed, the boys and girls did not shoot out the door as they normally did. One by one they came forward, bearing simple gifts for their teacher. Caroline was deeply touched as she accepted jars of watermelon pickles, blackberry jam, bouquets of wildflowers tied with string, shiny red apples, and tiny cakes made with white sugar. Polly had crocheted her a bookmark, and Maddy and her other friends had embroidered her initials on three new handkerchiefs.

"Goodness!" Caroline exclaimed in surprise. Tears of happiness welled in her eyes. "Thank you! Thank you all so much! You have made my first term teaching a memorable one!"

After everyone had gone and Eliza was helping Caroline tidy up by sweeping out the entryway, John came forward. He shyly held something out for Caroline. It was a long piece of green velvet ribbon that was faded and stained a little at the edges.

"I would like you to have that," he said.

"I know it's not much."

"Oh, John—" Caroline began. She knew instinctively that the ribbon must have belonged to his mother. Perhaps it was his only keepsake. She wanted to tell him that she could not possibly accept something this precious, but John spoke first.

"I know you didn't really need any help, Miss Quiner. I know you gave me these clothes I'm wearing because you are a good person." John looked down at the floor. "Because you are so good to me, I want to tell you something I did that was terrible, Miss Quiner."

He had spoken the last in a whisper, and Caroline had to lean forward a little to catch the words. He wore such an anguished expression on his young face, Caroline could not imagine what terrible thing it was he had done. She held her breath, waiting.

"I stole money from my pa," he said at last, and then he took a deep breath and rushed through his confession. "I stole it so I could come to school. I wanted to learn to read, but Pa always said it was a waste of money. But I think it's a waste what Pa does with it. He just buys liquor and drinks it till it's all gone. And so one night after he got paid, I waited till he had passed out drunk and I took the money that was left in his pockets. He thought he had lost it on the way home. And later I told him that the school lets some people come for free. So I stole and I lied, too!"

"I see," Caroline said softly, and then she was quiet, wondering what to do. She was surprised by John's actions. Part of her wanted to praise him for having the drive to come to school at all, but she knew she could not praise him for stealing and lying—even for a good reason.

"You understand what you did was wrong, don't you, John?" Caroline said at last.

John solemnly nodded.

"I cannot condone stealing and lying, for those are sins, John, and you must ask God's forgiveness for that," Caroline continued, choosing her words carefully. "I do admire your desire to learn and your perseverance, however. And I am proud of how hard you have worked to overcome adversity. Do you know what that word means, John? Adversity?"

"No, ma'am," John murmured, shaking his head.

"*Adversity* means misfortune or trouble—all the obstacles placed in the path of life. I think you've faced much adversity, John, in your young life. Despite that, you've shown a great deal of courage and dignity."

John began to sniffle a little, and he looked down at his shoes.

"It took courage to come to school," Caroline said. "And it will take courage to live an honest and truthful life. Promise me you will do that, John, no matter what obstacles you face."

"I promise, Miss Quiner!" John cried. "I will never lie or steal again."

"Good," Caroline said. "Now, John, I want you to know that you can always come to me with any troubles. I will do my best to help you."

"Thank you, Miss Quiner," John said, wiping the corners of his eyes. "I 'preciate what you've done for me and I'll never forget it as long as I live! That's why I want to give you that ribbon that belonged to my ma."

Caroline looked down at the ribbon, carefully smoothing it along the desk. "Thank you, John. I will cherish this gift always."

John turned then and hurried out the door, nearly colliding with Mr. Kellogg, who had just arrived.

"Beg your pardon, sir!" John said, dashing outside.

"Quite all right, young man," Mr. Kellogg replied, chuckling.

"Mr. Kellogg!" Caroline cried, standing up to greet him. "I'm so glad you're back from your travels. I trust everything went well."

"Yes, yes, Caroline, thank you," Mr. Kellogg answered, smiling. "Now I have come on your last day of school to congratulate you on a job well done, and to officially offer you the school next term."

"Oh, Mr. Kellogg, I happily accept your offer!" Caroline exclaimed. "It has been a pleasure to teach school."

"And I gather it's been a pleasure for our young scholars to have you as their teacher," Mr. Kellogg said. "Margaret speaks very highly of you, as do all your young charges. The members of the board have all had glowing reports from their children at home."

"Thank you," Caroline said, blushing. "The scholars were so good, it was easy to teach them."

"Well, no matter how good they were, children are children and must be handled properly, and that is just what you did," Mr. Kellogg said.

"Thank you, Mr. Kellogg!" Caroline repeated.

"Now then, I have something for you." Mr. Kellogg took a plain brown envelope from his pocket and handed it to Caroline.

Caroline knew it was her pay, and she couldn't wait to give it all to Mother and Pa. The money would be a great help to them.

Mr. Kellogg was about to take his leave when Caroline stopped him. "There is one thing I wish to discuss with you, Mr. Kellogg, if you have a moment."

"Of course, Caroline. What is it?" Mr. Kellogg asked.

"Did you notice the boy who was just leaving when you arrived?" Caroline began.

"Why, I couldn't miss him—he nearly knocked me down!" Mr. Kellogg laughed.

"I understand that his father works for you sometimes, at the inn. A Mr. Friday," Caroline continued.

"Oh, yes!" Mr. Kellogg's lips turned down in a frown. "But he's not a very reliable sort, I'm sorry to say. Has his son been giving you trouble at school?"

"Oh no," Caroline cried. "Quite the contrary." She took a deep breath and quickly explained about John and how much he had improved in such a short time. "He is such a diligent scholar," she said, summing it up. "But the boy has been horribly neglected, and I wonder if there is something you might do to help."

Caroline paused to gauge Mr. Kellogg's expression. He had brought a hand to his chin and appeared to be listening intently, so she continued.

"Young John is quite intelligent, Mr. Kellogg, and motivated. I think he would benefit from a good role model, not simply charity, because he is a proud little boy. I don't mean to be presumptuous, but I wondered if he could do some work for you or Mr. Larrimore. I'm sure he would be a willing and able worker, just as he has been a willing and able scholar."

Caroline came to the end of her speech, anxious to hear what Mr. Kellogg would say. She gazed tentatively up into his face and saw that now he looked very stern. Her heart gave a little leap inside her chest. What if she had offended him? Perhaps he would think she was just a busybody prying into other people's affairs.

"Goodness!" Mr. Kellogg cried at last. "I will of course look into the matter right away and see what is to be done for the poor boy. Mrs. Kellogg and I could use someone to carry bags and do odd jobs around our own home. If the boy is as able as you say, I'm sure he will like the work, and it will of course not be charity."

"Thank you again. Mr. Kellogg, I trusted you would know what to do," Caroline said. "And I doubt the boy will have money for school next term. He's very handy to me around here. Perhaps he could do chores at the school to earn his lessons. That is, if he's not too busy working for you."

"That sounds fine, Caroline," Mr. Kellogg said. Then he mused, "You are certainly a dedicated teacher, Caroline. I wonder if young Friday realizes how lucky he is."

As soon as Mr. Kellogg had left, Eliza came in from the entryway. Caroline was so happy, she pounced on her sister and gave her a great hug.

"Gracious, what's got into you all of a sudden!" Eliza exclaimed, giggling.

"Oh, I'm just so . . . happy!" Caroline cried. "Mr. Kellogg has agreed to help John."

"Yes, I know, I heard!" Eliza said.

"Eliza, you should never eavesdrop!" Caroline pretended to scold, smiling all the while.

"Well, I couldn't help it!" Eliza said. "I wasn't sure where else to go."

"Anyway, it doesn't matter. I'm just terribly relieved that Mr. Kellogg wants to help John," Caroline said.

"And you must be relieved that school is over," added Eliza.

"No, not really," Caroline confessed. "If it were up to me, I would have the school go all summer long."

"Well, I'm glad it's not up to you, then!" Eliza teased. "I can't wait to stay home for a whole month!"

Caroline playfully tweaked Eliza's nose, then turned to finish tidying the room, humming all the while. She was disappointed summer school was over, but nothing really could cloud the deep satisfaction she felt as she thought of all she had accomplished in three short months. Not only had her first term as a teacher been a success, she had earned money to help at home, and she had done what she had set out to do: help a young child in need.

A Dry Spell

On the first Monday home, Caroline felt a little like a ship adrift in the water with no wind under her sails. She missed the walk to Concord, the busyness of getting the schoolhouse ready for her scholars, and the fullness of her day as a teacher. But there was plenty to do around the house, of course, and soon Caroline settled back into her old routine.

She tended to the garden and helped with the preserving, canning the vegetables and making jams and pickles for the coming year.

She braided new hats for the whole family
from the straw Pa and Thomas cut, and she
plucked feathers from the ornery geese to
refill the pillows and comforters, making sure
to save some quills to use as pens for the next
term.

On her trips into town to the general store,
she would sometimes see John Friday. Mr.
Kellogg had been as good as his word, and
had given John work right away. John was
always busy and cheerful when she ran into
him on the street. Once or twice he had a
question from his primer, and she was glad to
see that he really was using what free time he
had to study.

The summer days continued to be hot
and terribly dry. The ground turned hard,
choking the plants. Caroline helped carry
bucket after bucket of water to the garden,
but the thirsty vegetables desperately
needed rain. The wheat crop was withering
in the heat as well.

In the evenings Pa did not smile very
much, and neither did Mother. Caroline

hated to see the worry in their eyes.

One night she overheard Mother ask Pa if he thought there would be any rain that week.

"No, Charlotte, I doubt it," Pa answered, and Caroline's heart sank. Pa was good at predicting weather. He could tell when it was going to rain because his bad legs would ache something awful, but he also watched for signs in the sky and studied the birds, plants, and animals in the woods. "I reckon we're going to have a dry spell, Charlotte," Pa said in his quiet, measured voice.

"Oh, Frederick," Mother sighed.

"We have money saved from last year's crop," Pa said then. "We'll make do, Charlotte. Try not to worry."

But Caroline could tell from the silence that Mother was worried, and so was she. And she decided to do something about it. That night when she was alone with her sisters, she asked Martha if she thought she could work extra hours for Widow Milton.

"Yes, she's always wanting me to," Martha

answered. "I was just going to suggest it to Mother myself."

"Well then, I wonder if there's any work for me while school is out," Caroline murmured, biting her lip.

Eliza's eyes lit up. "When I was at the store yesterday, I heard Mr. Jayson say he needed someone to make men's shirts!"

"Doesn't he have Mrs. Jenkins do that?" Caroline asked.

"Yes, but there are suddenly a lot more orders, on account of all the new settlers who are baching it," Eliza said.

"Oh, I hope he hasn't found anyone yet," Caroline exclaimed. "I'll go speak with him tomorrow."

"I could find some work too," Eliza offered.

Caroline shook her head. "If Martha and I are working out, you'll be needed here. You'll have to do extra chores."

"I don't mind," said Eliza. "And Lottie is such a big help now."

"Thank you!" Caroline gave Eliza a hug.

The very next morning after the chores

were done, Caroline slipped away to speak with Mr. Jayson. Luckily he had not found anyone to help with the sewing yet, and he was delighted that Caroline wanted the work. He would pay her fifty cents a shirt, a handsome sum. Right away he gave her a bolt of brown calico with an order for six work shirts to be completed as fast as she could.

When Caroline came home carrying the bolt of cloth, Mother was full of questions and then surprise as Caroline explained everything.

"What good girls I have," Mother said in a quiet voice. Caroline could tell she felt relieved. She knew Mother would never have asked her daughters to take on more work, but neither would she refuse the extra wages.

"Well, now that I have earned some money, I like the feeling," Caroline said, rolling out the calico onto the clean kitchen table to begin cutting out the shirts in the sizes Mr. Jayson had given her.

All that day and the next Caroline concentrated on her sewing, and she was able to bring the shirts to Mr. Jayson in just a few days' time.

"That was fast, young lady!" Mr. Jayson cried, eyes lighting up. "If you're willing and able, I'll take the same again!"

"Yes sir, I certainly am!" Caroline replied.

Mr. Jayson brought down another bolt of cloth, this time a blue calico. Then he counted out three silver dollars and handed them over.

The weight of the heavy coins inside her pocket and the sound of their jingling made Caroline feel like singing all the way home, and the look on Mother's face when she handed over the money was the best payment of all.

"Three whole dollars!" Eliza cried when she came in from her chores "Maybe you'd rather be a dressmaker like Mother instead of teaching school!"

Caroline shook her head. She had never liked to sew, even though Mother had made sure that all her girls could do it well. It was such slow and exacting work, bending over the needle, trying to make the stitches tiny and neat. Caroline had learned to be quick because she wanted the work to be over, but how much quicker she would be if she had one of those newfangled sewing machines! She had seen one at a dressmaker's shop in Milwaukee and had watched in amazement as the seamstress had sewn up a bodice in no time flat. With a sewing machine, Caroline would be able do the work for Mr. Jayson in half the time and earn twice the money. But wishing for a sewing machine was like wishing for a piece of cheese from the moon, as Henry liked to say. No one Caroline knew in Concord owned a sewing machine.

All that week and the next there were more orders. Caroline's fingers ached from holding the needle, and her neck was sore from bending over her sewing. Still, it was all worth it to see Mother's happy face when Caroline handed over the silver dollars.

With September a little rain came at last— enough to give the land a good drink, though not enough to save the crop entirely.

A Dry Spell

On the Friday before the fall term was set to begin, Caroline took a bundle of shirts to Mr. Jayson.

"The orders have slowed down a bit, but they might start up again when it turns cold," Mr. Jayson said. "You've done such marvelous work, I may need to call on you again. Would that be all right?"

"Yes, of course, Mr. Jayson, that would be fine," Caroline said, happily taking her final pay. She would gladly have sewn during recess and in the evenings after school, but she felt relieved to have a respite. Now she could concentrate all her attention on teaching once more.

A New Term Begins

On Monday morning, Caroline was so excited she was going to school, she jumped out of bed and hurried to get dressed, humming all the while. It was a first day yet again, and she was a little jittery as she walked to school with Eliza, but not nearly as much as before.

John Friday was the first to arrive after Caroline had unlocked the schoolhouse door. He was clean from head to toe and he had his own dinner pail, which he proudly set on the shelf in the entryway.

"Mrs. Larrimore says I am to come home to the inn for dinner most days, but I told her that you would probably need my help today, being it's the first day and all," John announced.

"Oh, John, thank you, that is very considerate of you," Caroline said. She knew from Mr. Kellogg that the Larrimores had taken a particular liking to John once he had started working at the inn every day. They had no children of their own, and they had offered to pay for his schooling themselves so John would not have to do extra work around the school unless he wanted to.

"Should I fetch the water for you, Miss Quiner?" John asked.

"Yes, that would be nice, John, thank you," Caroline answered warmly. She was extremely happy with how things had turned out.

When it was a quarter to nine, the other scholars began to arrive and the rows of desks quickly filled. Just as Caroline had anticipated, there were many new faces among the familiar ones. By the time she stood to ring the bell, only the back two rows were empty, and those would be full come winter when the big boys returned to school from working in the fields.

It took nearly an hour to write down the names and ages of all the new scholars, and to find out where they were in their studies. There were three new girls about her own age and nearly a dozen younger girls and boys.

Right away Caroline saw that teaching a larger school would not be easy. It would take more time to organize the different classes and to assign the lessons and check all the work. The boys and girls who had been with her in the summer were quiet and diligent, but many of the new scholars were undisciplined and unruly.

By the time she dismissed the room for morning recess, Caroline had already had to speak sternly to several boys. Two brothers, Abe and Jack Dawson, aged twelve and thirteen, were particularly mischievous. They fidgeted, whispered, and poked at each other until finally Caroline had to separate them.

After that things went more smoothly for a

time, until Caroline had to reprimand two girls about Eliza's age who were giggling and passing notes. Then she had to stop two brothers from bickering over the primer they were sharing.

At noon recess Caroline was distracted as she sat with her friends. She could tell Polly and Maddy wanted to cheer her, but Caroline's thoughts kept straying to the lessons, wondering how she could organize everything more efficiently.

All through arithmetic there were thankfully no disruptions. Then during grammar, when Caroline was working with the younger class, a girl named Emily Jackson suddenly jumped up from her seat and began wailing.

"Oh! Oh! Oh!" the girl cried, turning in circles and trying to reach for something behind her.

Caroline was so startled, she simply stared at the girl for a moment; then she rushed to Emily and took hold of her. She saw that something was moving inside the back collar of Emily's dress. She reached down and pulled out a small green frog.

There was a burst of laughter and then deadly silence as Caroline briskly took the frog outside, returned, and surveyed the room with her sternest expression.

"Do you know who did this, Emily?" Caroline asked.

Emily shook her head, but Abe Dawson, who was sitting directly behind the girl, began to shake uncontrollably with pent-up laughter.

Caroline knew it had been Abe who had caused the mischief. She felt her cheeks blush pink as the anger rose within her. She would have to punish the boy, but she hated to use the cane, as Mr. Linney would have done.

"Abe Dawson, please come and stand before me," she said in her sternest voice, and after he had trudged up front, she continued. "You have disrupted the entire school, and you have been unkind to a fellow classmate. Therefore, you must stand and face that corner until I dismiss you."

Abe trudged to the corner and Caroline

went back to teaching, but the new scholars were restless, watching Abe. And Abe kept turning and making faces during lessons, which made Caroline nearly lose her temper and cane the boy anyway; but she caught herself just in time. For the first time in her short life as a teacher, Caroline could not wait for the school day to end.

At last the terrible day was over and Caroline was glad. She dismissed the school, all except for Abe, who had to stay and write on the board "I will not disrupt school" fifty times.

"Can I go home now, Miss Quiner?" he asked as soon as he was done.

"May I go home," Caroline corrected.

"May I?" Abe repeated.

"Yes, Abe," Caroline answered. "But if you disrupt school again tomorrow, just once, I will keep you in at recess this whole week."

"Yes, ma'am," Abe mumbled, and then dashed out the door.

Caroline gave a little sigh and sank down into her chair. How different this first day was from the last! She felt weary instead of invigorated, and she was glad that Eliza had gone home already and John had left so they could not see her this defeated.

You were just lucky the first time, Caroline thought. *This is what teaching school is really like.*

She couldn't help but wonder if she was really up to the challenge of teaching a larger school. Maybe she was too young to manage, as Martha had suggested. What if the scholars became more and more unruly? What if she could not handle them all?

During summer school she had taken Miss May's example and tried to engage the scholars rather than bully them into learning. This mild approach had worked on the younger scholars in a smaller school, but what if it didn't work now? What if she lost control completely? Then the board would have no choice but to dismiss her from her post.

Caroline imagined the looks of disappointment on the faces of those she admired the most: Mr. Kellogg and her own mother. How awful it would be to fail when everyone—the town and her family—was counting on her to succeed.

"You cannot fail! You will not!" she said out loud. "You had one bad day and that is all. You are just feeling sorry for yourself, Caroline Lake Quiner."

With that she stood and cleaned the blackboard, swept the floors, and straightened the desks. When the school was tidy, she put on her jacket and bonnet and locked the door behind her.

At home Mother's eyes were full of concern, because Eliza had already told about the troubles at school. Caroline would have broken down right then and there if she had not had the whole walk through the woods to compose herself.

"It was not an ideal first day," Caroline admitted, "but I can't expect teaching to always be easy. It will just take a little getting used to, managing a larger school, that is all. Summer school was so simple, I was not prepared for how unruly the older boys could be. Now I am."

Truthfully, Caroline knew she sounded more confident than she felt. But sounding brave was a step toward being brave, she decided. She must keep a positive attitude and never ever again give in to self-pity, as she had briefly done at school.

The next morning Caroline awoke early as usual, dressed with purpose, and headed to school, forcing herself to ignore the tiny doubts that kept creeping into her mind.

John was at the schoolhouse already, and though he did not say anything about the previous day, it was obvious that he was trying to make her feel better by helping in whatever way he could.

"You are such a thoughtful boy, John," Caroline told him after he had come back from fetching the water. "I do appreciate all you do around here."

John shrugged. "Aw, I don't do that much. Nothing compared to what you did for me—teaching me to read and write and all."

With John's words Caroline felt her confidence return. She had not had to bully John into learning, after all. Perhaps there was a way to be strong and gentle at once. She never wanted to whip the children to make them mind, but neither could she allow them to walk all over her.

All that day, and for the whole week, Caroline vigilantly watched for any disruption, no matter how small or innocent. Then she was quick to mete out punishment—extra homework or detention, not whippings. At the same time she praised and rewarded the good behavior of others with high marks and special treats like being able to copy their work on the board for all to see.

Day by day there were fewer and fewer outbursts. Jack Dawson kept trying to provoke his brother into mischief, and Caroline could see that Abe *wanted* to misbehave, but the threat of going for an entire week without recess kept the boy reined in like a colt in its first harness.

And Caroline was surprised to discover that both boys were good scholars when they actually concentrated on their lessons. So she gave them a great deal of praise when they did well, and it seemed to work like a charm. Instead of each trying to outdo the other with pranks, they began to compete to see who could get the best marks.

At the end of the week Caroline was exhausted—more exhausted than she had ever been during summer school. But she was triumphant as well. It was one week she had managed and not failed, and slowly she found that she did not have to try so hard. The seeds of discipline she was sowing began to sprout and grow.

A Surprise Meeting

One late October morning, as Caroline stood packing the dinner pail, Mother said, "I can tell things are going well at school because your eyes are happy again."

Caroline was surprised by Mother's words. She had worked hard during the past weeks never to appear discouraged at school or at home, even after the most trying of days.

"I know you very well, Caroline," Mother continued. "You would never complain, but I understand it hasn't been easy, and I am proud of you for sticking with teaching no matter what."

"I do love teaching school, Mother," Caroline said, and as she spoke the words, she realized that they were true again. She had been concentrating so hard on not failing, she hadn't even known that her love of teaching had blossomed again like a late-blooming rose.

That day, as a kind of celebration, she let the whole school play multiplication games and word games, something she had hardly done all term because she had not trusted them. There were no outbursts all morning and afternoon, and by four o'clock Caroline was so pleased with her scholars, she could have taken flight if she'd had wings.

"No one must stay in detention today," she happily announced after she had brought the room to order. "Go home and enjoy yourselves. I shall see you all again Monday."

Eliza left as soon as Caroline rang the bell, because Mother was busy with canning. John was needed at the inn, as the stagecoach came that day, so he said good-bye as well. Caroline cleaned the schoolroom by herself, locked it, and set off toward home.

The days had grown short, and the sun was just beginning to set with a burst of brilliant pink in the western sky. The shadows were long as Caroline turned onto Main Street. In Milwaukee at this time of night, the lamplighters would be going through the streets lighting the lamps. But here in Concord there were no streetlamps, just the cheery lights from the windows of the inn and the shops.

It had remained unseasonably warm all through September, and even into October. Now there was a chill in the air and Caroline wrapped her woolen shawl a little tighter about her shoulders. She was just passing the general store when Mr. Jayson came outside and beckoned to her.

"Excuse me, Caroline, I've been watching for you. I have more orders for shirts, if you can take them—four shirts same cut as before."

"Yes, I'd be happy to, Mr. Jayson," Caroline said, and followed him into the store.

"I'll just finish some business with this

young man here and then give you the cloth,"
Mr. Jayson told her.

When Caroline reached the counter, she
was surprised to see that the young man was
Charles Ingalls. He swept the hat from his
head and smiled down at her. "Why, hello,
Caroline. How do you do?"

Caroline felt herself blushing a little, and
she supposed it was at the surprise of seeing
Charles again after so many months. His thick
brown hair had been cut short, and his clean-
shaven face was still brown from the summer
months.

"Polly didn't mention you had come back
again," Caroline said.

"Only just arrived," Charles replied. "I am
on my way home now."

"Now then, Ingalls, here we are!" Mr. Jayson
spoke up. He set a flat package wrapped in
brown paper on the counter. "This is the item
you ordered back in July, and I'll just wrap up
the sugar and coffee for you as well."

"You can see to the lady first," Charles gra-
ciously offered.

Caroline smiled to herself. It was strange to be called a "lady" by Charles Ingalls.

"Capital idea, young man!" Mr. Jayson cried. He brought down a bolt of red cloth and some black buttons in a paper packet. "There you go, Caroline. A nice, warm wool for the winter months."

"Thank you again, Mr. Jayson." Caroline reached for the cloth, but Charles intercepted it.

"Since we're both going in the same direction, I'll carry it for you," he said.

"But you have your own packages to carry," Caroline protested. "And besides, you don't need to go as far as my house."

"I don't mind," Charles replied.

It would be rude to protest further, so Caroline smiled and said, "Thank you. It's very kind of you." She waited while Mr. Jayson finished wrapping Charles's packages and marking them in the account book, and then the two set off toward Territorial Road.

The sky had burned an even deeper shade of pink—it was nearly red.

"'Red sky at night, sailors' delight,'"

Charles quoted the old saying.

"And farmers' delight too," Caroline added.

Charles laughed. "You're right about that. It turned into a nice fall, but it's too bad we didn't have more rain this summer."

"Yes, our wheat crop was nearly lost," Caroline said.

"It was the same for Peter and me—and Pa, too," Charles said.

On Territorial Road wagons and buggies rolled noisily by, so it was impossible to speak for a time. Caroline was glad. She could not think of a thing to say. She had seldom been alone with Charles over the years, and he was a grown man now. She wasn't sure what to talk about.

Then she remembered how she had wished to compliment him on his fiddle playing back in July. When the road was clear again, she said, "I so enjoyed the music you played on Independence Day. I wanted to tell you then, but never had the chance."

"Thank you," Charles replied. "I was happy to do my part to make the festivities more jolly."

"Oh, you made them jolly indeed," Caroline enthused. "Polly says you can pick up a tune after hearing it once."

"Well, it takes a bit of practice to make the song worth hearing," Charles answered modestly.

"Still, it must be nice to play an instrument," Caroline persisted. "You can always entertain yourself when you're alone."

"True enough. I do that for my brother and myself at his cabin up north. It's a lonely place, but Peter likes it that way, and so do I." He paused and then quickly added, "Except, of course, I like good company, too."

Caroline felt herself blushing again at Charles's compliment. She was glad that it was dusk and her bonnet hid most of her face.

After two more wagons had jingled by, Charles held up the bolt of cloth he was carrying and said, "Fixing to make yourself a new dress?"

"Oh, no," Caroline answered. "I am making shirts for Mr. Jayson to sell."

"A seamstress as well as a schoolteacher. I guess you like to keep busy!" Charles said. "I do too. Peter and I have a little business up north, besides the farming. We do hauling for folks who don't have their own wagon. We haul a lot of logs to the railroad, let me tell you."

"Joseph and Henry do the same thing," Caroline said. "Henry wants to save his money to go out west one day."

"That's my plan too," Charles said.

Caroline did not tell him that she had already heard this from Polly. "Where do you plan to go? California?" she asked instead.

Charles shook his head. "Naw. I'm not so interested in gold. And besides, I hear the gold's mostly dried up now. No, I'd like to go to where the land is rich and free for the taking and no trees as far as the eye can see. If I never see another tree to chop, I'll die a happy man."

Charles sounded just like Henry. Henry had spent nearly his entire young life clearing trees for farmland, and Charles probably had too. Caroline knew that the western plains were supposed to be like vast oceans of grass with hardly a single tree anywhere, but it was hard to imagine such a place.

"I was thinking of Dakota Territory or Kansas," Charles continued.

"Bloody Kansas," Caroline said, and could not help but shudder a little.

Kansas was called "Bloody" because of all the fighting and blood spilling over the issue of slavery, of making the state free or slave-holding. Caroline had learned a great deal about the place when she had lived in Milwaukee, because her uncle owned a newspaper and printed stories for the abolitionist cause.

"I admire the men who go to Kansas to fight for the cause of freedom," Caroline said. "But it's certainly not a place for women and children to settle."

"I guess it's a rough place at that," Charles admitted.

They were quiet again as they turned onto the path leading into the woods. Under the canopy of trees it was darker, though the reddish-purple sky could still be seen through the leaves overhead. As they walked, the squirrels and chipmunks rustled in the brush and crisscrossed the path, madly hunting for nuts to store away for winter. The birds in the tall branches were singing their last songs before night fell completely.

"Sure gets dark fast these days," Charles said. "You don't mind walking home by yourself?"

"Eliza is often with me, and sometimes we walk partway with Polly and Docia," Caroline said. "But no, I don't mind walking alone. I wasn't born in the woods to be scared by an owl."

Charles let out a short, quick laugh. "That's what my ma says too."

Soon they came to the cutoff that led across the creek to the Ingallses' land.

"You really don't have to walk me all the way," Caroline said.

"I don't mind," Charles answered. Caroline was glad they were not parting ways yet. She discovered she liked talking with Charles. It was as easy as talking with her own brothers, but it was different too.

"What do you think I have here?" Charles asked then, interrupting Caroline's thoughts. He held up the package from the general store.

"Goodness, I could not begin to guess," Caroline said.

"It's a book," Charles announced. "A book about nature and animals. Mr. Jayson ordered it for me when I was here in July, and it just came in. You see, I like to keep my mind occupied too!"

"You ordered a book?" Caroline could not hide her amazement.

"What, you don't think a fella likes to read now and again?" Charles cried, pretending to be offended.

"I am sorry, Charles," Caroline quickly said. "I guess I *am* a little surprised. It's just that, well, I can't see Henry or Joseph spending their hard-earned money on a book."

"I like to read," Charles said with a grin. "I guess you do too?"

"It's one of my favorite things to do, when

I have the time," Caroline replied warmly. "A good book makes me feel as if I have traveled to another place and time altogether, but I never have to leave my own home."

Charles nodded. "I know what you mean. Though I like the idea of traveling in real life, not just in books."

Caroline was about to ask what authors Charles had read and what books he liked best when she realized they had come to the clearing already.

"Here we are," Charles said as they stepped out of the woods. "Home sweet home."

"Yes," Caroline answered. She was sorry the walk had come to an end, and she wondered if Charles felt the same way. He seemed to hesitate before handing over the bolt of cloth. "Thank you again for carrying this for me," she added.

"You are quite welcome," Charles said. He stood for a moment longer, gazing up at the trees and back down at the ground. At last he gave Caroline a quick smile and tipped his hat.

"Well, then, I guess I'll say good night, Caroline."

"Good night, Charles," Caroline replied.

Charles headed back toward the path, but stopped and waved before disappearing completely into the dark of the woods.

Caroline stood for a moment in the twilight. The moon had risen over the tops of the trees, and the North Star was twinkling overhead. As she walked across the clearing, Caroline began to hum. She was just passing the chicken coop when there was a rustling and something rushed out of the shadows.

"Was that Charles Ingalls who walked you home from town?" a voice whispered excitedly, and a hand grabbed Caroline by the arm.

"Eliza! You scared me nearly to death!" Caroline cried; then she pretended to grow stern. "Were you eavesdropping?"

"I was just seeing to the chickens," Eliza quickly replied, "and then you appeared with your secret beau!"

"Secret beau!" Caroline said with a laugh. "You certainly have a vivid imagination."

"Well, what was Charles doing walking you home?" Eliza persisted.

"He was at the store when Mr. Jayson gave me this cloth to make more shirts, so he offered to carry it for me since we were going the same way. That is all!"

Eliza seemed greatly disappointed. "Well, Charles is awfully handsome, I've always thought. I used to be sweet on him when I was little, on account of his smile. It's a nice smile, don't you think?"

Caroline just shook her head at her sister's chattering. Eliza could be such a little squirrel at times. "All the Ingallses have nice smiles," Caroline lightly answered. "Polly has a lovely smile, and so does Docia."

"But I wasn't talking about Polly or Docia," Eliza said, taking Caroline's hand and squeezing it. "Oh, Caroline, wouldn't it be wonderful if Charles started courting you!"

"Eliza, you can be very silly! Very silly indeed!" Caroline said. "You seem to want me to do everything but teach school. You'd have me be a dressmaker or a married lady before I'm even eighteen years old. But I told you before, I like teaching school. And I don't want anyone courting me just yet, thank you very much."

"Not even someone as handsome and nice as Charles Ingalls?" Eliza said with a smile.

"Not even Charles Ingalls," Caroline answered.

The Cornhusking

A utumn was always the busiest time around the farm. Even though the crops had suffered from the drought, there was still a great deal to do to get ready for winter.

After the wheat had been cut and dried, it had to be threshed and packed into burlap sacks to be taken to sell at the mill. The potatoes had to be stored away in a potato pit that Pa had dug and lined with straw near the cellar. The late vegetables like pumpkins and squash were stewed and canned. A hog was butchered, the meat smoked, and the grease made into soap and enough candles for the whole year.

When the sisters were alone together, going about their chores before and after school, Eliza often teased Caroline about Charles. He had come home to stay for the winter, and so Caroline saw him when she visited Polly, and at church on Sundays. They always exchanged a few pleasant words, but that was all. Caroline knew from what Polly had said that Charles was not interested in finding a wife, and she certainly was not interested in being one yet. But it seemed to give Eliza great pleasure to make a mountain out of a molehill, and she always reported back to Caroline if she had caught even the slightest glimpse of Charles about town.

One Thursday evening Eliza came to Caroline and said, "Wouldn't you like to hear Charles play his fiddle again?"

"Everyone likes to hear a fiddle when it is played well," Caroline replied matter-of-factly.

"Well, you'll get the chance tomorrow

night! Docia told me that Mr. Spivey has asked Charles to play at his cornhusking! Won't that be fun!"

"It's always nice to have music at a husking," Caroline answered in the same even tone, but deep down she did feel a tingle of excitement.

It was the time of year when farmers all about Concord were hosting work parties of one kind or another. There had already been a threshing and a hog killing. Neighbors brought food and visited together. Many hands made the work go quicker, and so did music. A cornhusking often turned into a dance at the end of the evening if there was a fiddler about.

"Maybe you'll get to dance with Charles!" Eliza said.

"Now, how can I do that, when he will be the one doing the fiddling?" Caroline laughed.

"Well, maybe you'll get the red ear while Charles is sitting next to you," Eliza said slyly.

At a husking, finding a red ear of corn among the yellow and white ears meant that a boy or girl, man or woman, had to kiss the person sitting beside them. Finding a blackened ear meant a playful slap instead of a kiss. The game was supposed to be a courting game, and Caroline thought it was all very silly, but she tried to mind whom she sat next to all the same. She would hate to have to kiss a strange man. And it would be terribly embarrassing to be made to kiss someone familiar, too, like Charles. Her cheeks burned a little at the thought.

"The only ear I'm going to get is yours, Eliza Quiner, and it will be red when I'm finished with it!" Caroline reached for Eliza's ear to mockingly pinch it, but Eliza dashed away, giggling.

When Friday evening came around, the sisters dressed in their nicest everyday dresses, but not their Sunday best. It was dusty work, sitting in a barn, separating the ears of corn from their crisp husks and golden tassels. It was chilly work too. There was a thin coat of snow on the ground already, and the evening was bitterly cold. Caroline put on her red-

and-black plaid wool dress and wore her thickest shawl.

Downstairs, Joseph and Henry had arrived while the girls were dressing, and so had Charlie Carpenter, who had come all the way from Brookfield. The young men were all standing around the fire in the kitchen, chatting with Thomas and Pa.

Charlie would take Martha to the husking in his buggy, and Thomas, Joseph, and Henry would escort Caroline and Eliza in the wagon. Pa was not going, because his legs were aching from the cold, and Mother had decided that she and Lottie would stay home with him, even though Lottie had put up quite a fuss because she hated to be left out of anything.

"Spivey has a heap of corn, even with the dry weather!" Joseph was saying as the girls came downstairs.

"Is that so?" Pa said. "Well, good for him."

"Hey, that smells mighty good!" Henry said, following Caroline to the shelf where her apple pie was cooling. "Did you make that?"

Caroline nodded, and Henry said, "I could eat the whole thing myself. I sure do like your pies."

"'Hunger makes the best sauce,'" Caroline quoted as she wrapped the pie in a clean dish towel. "Why, you and Joseph are as thin as rails! What do you two cook for yourselves?"

"Squirrel meat mostly," Henry answered.

"You know you boys can come here for supper anytime you please," Mother said from where she was knitting by the fire. "I want you and Joseph to get enough to eat."

"We know, Mother," Henry said. "We just don't want to be a burden."

"Of course you wouldn't be a burden!" Mother cried. "I don't know where you get such foolish ideas."

"We'd better head out before we get too cozy," Joseph said then. "It's a mighty cold night for a party."

"My legs tell me there's going to be a heap more snow before morning," Pa said. "I want you boys to be careful and bring the girls home before it gets too late."

"Goodness, maybe they shouldn't go at all, Frederick, if you think it's going to be bad!" Mother fretted, standing to look out the window.

"Oh, Mother!" Eliza cried. "Please, we have to go! The whole town will be there, and Charles is going to play the fiddle, and we'll be able to dance."

Mother looked uncertain, and Caroline was surprised to feel her own heart sinking a little. She was looking forward to the husking mainly, she realized, because of Charles and his fiddle.

"I think it's all right, Charlotte," Pa said. "Just make sure you keep a watch on the weather, boys, and head home at the first sign of snow."

"Yessir, we will," Joseph and Henry and Charlie all promised before heading out into the cold to get the oxen ready.

Caroline buttoned her coat over her shawl and turned to say good-bye to Lottie, who was pouting by the fire.

The Cornhusking

"We'll make you a cornhusk dolly, how about that?" Caroline said, giving Lottie a kiss on the cheek.

Lottie's blue eyes brightened. "Do you promise?"

"Yes, I do," Caroline said.

Mother gave Caroline and Martha and Eliza the potatoes she had heated in the stove to put inside their coat pockets. Then she helped wrap the woolen mufflers about their heads and faces.

"Remember what your pa said!" Mother told them. "You must be sure to come home before the bad weather starts."

"We will, Mother," the girls answered all together.

Outside, the cold took Caroline's breath away. She hurried into the back of the wagon with Eliza, and they wrapped the woolen blankets about themselves.

Martha waved from Charlie's buggy as the horse took off at a fast trot over the hard, frozen ground. The oxen Joseph was driving were no match for one young horse pulling a light buggy. Martha and Charlie were soon lost from sight.

In the clearing the black sky twinkled with stars. It was a beautifully clear night and terribly cold. No clouds and too cold for snow. Maybe Pa had been wrong about the weather, Caroline thought.

Once they were on the path, the wind whistled through the woods. Most trees, except for the tall pines, had lost their leaves by now. The bare branches appeared menacing in the pale moonlight, especially the sycamores, with their white arms reaching out like ghosts in the darkened forest.

Caroline shivered. Her hands were warm as she held the potatoes, but her face was cold. She tucked her chin down into her muffler and closed her eyes.

She listened to the jingle of the harness, the creak of the wheels, and the measured plod of the oxen treading on hard ground. Except for the wind in the trees, there seemed to be no other sound. All the creatures of the woods had hidden away from the cold.

The Cornhusking

It was nearly eight miles to Mr. Spivey's house, and the time passed slowly. At last Caroline heard the friendly sound of voices. She opened her eyes to see that they were coming into the Spiveys' yard. The clearing was filled with horses and wagons and buggies. One great door of the barn had been slid open to let in newcomers, and the yellow light was a beacon in the night.

"Welcome, welcome!" Mr. Spivey was calling from the doorway. "I'm mighty grateful to you folks for coming out on such a cold night."

The boys stayed outside to tend to the oxen, but Caroline and Eliza rushed inside, where it was bright and cheerful and delightfully warm. A potbellied stove glowed in one corner, and lanterns hung from the rafters. Children played tag around the tall mountain of corn rising up from the hard dirt floor. A group of young boys darted among the hay bales, chasing young girls and trying to throw yellow corn tassels into their hair.

The grown-ups stood in little groups visiting with one another, so the room buzzed with talk and laughter. Eliza had been right. Most of the town was in attendance. The Kelloggs greeted Caroline and Eliza after they had removed their coats, as did the Larrimores and the Jaysons.

Mr. Ingalls was there, and so was his wife, holding a sleeping baby Lansford in her arms. They greeted the girls warmly and asked after their family.

"I will send over a special ointment to rub on his legs," Mrs. Ingalls said when she heard that Pa's legs were poorly. "Your mother told me it helped last time."

"Yes, it did, thank you, Mrs. Ingalls," Caroline answered. The Ingallses were such good neighbors, always ready to lend a helping hand.

"Is Charles here? We heard he was playing fiddle tonight," Eliza asked, glancing sideways at Caroline.

"Yes, that's right, young lady! He's around here somewhere," Mr. Ingalls answered, waving a hand in the air. His face crinkled into a smile, and Caroline realized that his eyes were the same bold blue as his son's.

The Cornhusking

The Ingallses turned to greet another couple, and Eliza went to find her friends. Caroline took her pie to the long plank table running the length of one wall. The table was already laden with pots of beans, sweet potatoes, hulled corn, stewed carrots, and pumpkin; pans of corn bread, spoon bread, and pudding; platters of roast beef and venison, smoked ham and turkey; and all kinds of pickles, from beets to okra. There were also a number of scrumptious-looking pies, and Caroline set hers among them.

"Good evening, Caroline." Mrs. Spivey came up beside her then, lips turned down in a habitual frown. "You brought a pie, I see. It's not dried cherry, is it? Dried cherry is my favorite."

"Good evening, Mrs. Spivey," Caroline politely replied. "No, it's apple, ma'am. I'm afraid we didn't have any dried cherries."

"Oh well, an apple pie is nice enough, I suppose." Mrs. Spivey sighed. "I do hope there will be enough to feed everyone. I don't know why Mr. Spivey picked such a terrible night for a husking!"

"I suppose Mr. Spivey couldn't help the weather," Caroline said as brightly as she could. She had never liked Mrs. Spivey, because she was so sour and always complaining about one thing or another. "It's nice that so many have come out despite the cold," Caroline said cheerfully.

"Well, the cold kept a few away," Mrs. Spivey replied, glancing about the room. "I see your folks did not make the trip."

Caroline pursed her lips and made herself keep quiet. Mrs. Spivey could be terribly rude! Caroline would have liked to say something rude back, but she knew it was important to be polite no matter what. Meet opposition with cheerfulness, Mother often said.

"Mother was sorry she could not come, but Pa did not feel well tonight, and she thought it best to stay home to tend to him," Caroline explained.

"I do not feel well myself. My rheumatism is acting up again, but here I am!" Mrs. Spivey said. Then she abruptly turned to greet another new arrival. Caroline was relieved to be dismissed.

"Unpleasant old biddy!" Martha quietly hissed. She had come up beside Caroline without her knowing it.

"Martha, don't be mean!" Caroline scolded, but not very forcefully. In all the years she had known Mrs. Spivey, Caroline did not think she had once seen the woman smile, not even at the wedding of her own daughter, Nell. It was a testament to Mr. Spivey's character that he never succumbed to his wife's nagging nature and always seemed pleasant and jolly. And it was a wonder that Nell was as sweet as a girl could be.

"Where is Nell? Did she come out tonight?" Caroline asked now. "I haven't seen the baby in so long."

"She's right over there," Martha said, nodding toward one corner of the barn, where a group of their friends had gathered among the hay bales, cooing over Nell's little boy.

"He's grown so big!" Polly was saying as Caroline and Martha joined them.

"And look at those beautiful curls!" Maddy cried.

"How handsome he looks, Nell!" Caroline said.

The boy was six months old now, with round cheeks and big brown eyes and curly brown hair. His chubby fist grabbed at Caroline's finger when she held it out to him.

"He's strong, too!" She laughed.

"Strong, yes, and willful, that's for certain," Nell said. "He just about wears me out." But Caroline thought she did not look worn out at all. Her pretty face was glowing, and she seemed perfectly content. How different she was from her mother!

"I hear that fiddling brother of yours is going to play for us," Maddy said, turning to Polly. "I hope so, because I do feel like dancing, especially when there are so many young bachelors around."

Maddy and the other girls giggled. Caroline turned to glance at the crowd. She did not know many of the young men milling about, but she did recognize several shirts as the very ones she had made for Mr. Jayson.

"Charles is going to play, sure enough," Polly said, "but I reckon we'll have to get through all that corn before any dancing is to be done tonight!"

Now they all turned to look at the mountain of corn. Already people were finding seats among the hay bales and settling in to begin the husking.

"We'd best get to it, girls, if there's to be any dancing at all this evening!" Martha said. Then she gave a wry smile and added, "I know who I'm sitting next to tonight, but I guess you girls will have to take care!"

"Oh, let's sit all together!" Polly cried.

"That's no fun!" Maddy scoffed.

"I'll sit next to you, Polly!" Caroline said, thinking again of how embarrassing it would be to find a red ear of corn while sitting next to someone like Charles.

Thinking of Charles made Caroline glance around the room once more looking for him. This time she found him in a corner talking with Henry and Joseph and Thomas.

Like everyone else Charles was dressed for work, but he looked especially handsome in his neat brown trousers and crisp blue calico shirt and a black wool vest. His thick brown hair had been slicked down. He was laughing at something Henry had just said.

At that very moment Charles's bright-blue eyes swept the room and caught Caroline watching him. He grinned and nodded to her and she smiled back, but her face felt stiff and she knew she was blushing. Quickly she glanced away, feeling very silly. She wondered what Charles could possibly think of her when she always seemed to be blushing around him.

Caroline saw that Polly had already found a hay bale close to the mountain of corn, so she moved to join her friend but found her way suddenly blocked by Mr. Linney.

"Good evening, Miss Quiner," Mr. Linney said, giving a formal little bow. He was dressed in a nice brown suit instead of work clothes, and Caroline wondered if he had ever been to a husking before. She had certainly never seen him at one.

"Why, good evening, Mr. Linney," Caroline replied.

"Tell me, are you finding being a school-teacher to your liking?" he asked.

"Yes, I am, Mr. Linney, thank you," Caroline said.

"Not having any trouble then, making the boys mind you, Miss Quiner?" Mr. Linney asked.

"I must admit I have found the fall term to be more of a challenge than the summer term, but I am happy to say that I have been able to manage well enough," Caroline answered.

"Boys need discipline! That's the key. Discipline!" Mr. Linney intoned. "They must be made to mind. But I don't want to give you advice when you obviously do not need it. I hear glowing reports, glowing indeed!"

"Why, thank you, Mr. Linney, that is very kind of you to say. But of course I would always value your good advice," Caroline said politely. She paused, thinking Mr. Linney meant to exchange a few pleasantries and then excuse himself, but he remained standing before her.

"May I escort you to a seat, Miss Quiner?" Mr. Linney asked then.

"Well, I . . ." Caroline hesitated. She did not want to be rude, but neither did she want to sit next to Mr. Linney. "Thank you, Mr. Linney . . . but I—"

"Very good, then," Mr. Linney said. He had obviously taken her thanks as a yes. Before she knew it, she had been guided to a hay bale, and Mr. Linney had taken the seat beside her!

"Will this do, Miss Quiner?" Mr. Linney asked.

In a kind of daze, Caroline answered, "Yes, thank you, Mr. Linney." Helplessly she glanced back at Martha and Polly and her friends. They were all watching her with surprise and not a little amusement at her predicament.

Caroline swallowed hard and felt her cheeks flushing anew. What if she found a red ear of corn now? She would be expected to kiss Mr. Linney!

Skinny Linney.

The words came to her before she could stop them, and she felt a burst of anger at her old teacher. What did the man mean by sitting beside her? Did he not know about the kissing game? Could he possibly be interested in courting her? That was often what it meant when an unmarried man went out of his way to take a seat next to a particular young lady.

The idea of Mr. Linney being interested in her as a wife seemed so preposterous, Caroline nearly laughed out loud. Then she wondered with a start what others would think of Mr. Linney approaching her. What would Charles think? She glanced about the room, but Charles was gone from his spot, nowhere to be seen. And no one else seemed to be paying her any mind. Everyone was busy husking corn now.

"I am afraid I am not very good at this," Mr. Linney said, picking up an ear of corn. "It's my first husking."

Caroline's anger and distress began to subside as she watched Mr. Linney fumble to remove the husk. His hands were still as delicate and callus free as she remembered them from school. She doubted he had done much work himself since buying a farm. Maybe he was lonely. He had always seemed awkward about town when he was not teaching school. He was like a fish out of water, Caroline decided. He had given up his post but remained in Concord. And he had bought property but did not appear to be much of a farmer. Most likely he did not know about the silly kissing game. He had simply wished to talk to Caroline because she was familiar and they shared a common interest: school.

"It's easy once you get the hang of it, Mr. Linney," Caroline said in a friendly tone. She took up an ear of corn, quickly shucked it, and threw the dry husk to one side and the freed cob to the other.

"I see you are quite good at this, Miss Quiner. I shall study your technique a moment, if you don't mind," Mr. Linney said.

A tiny laugh escaped Caroline's lips. "I am not sure how much technique is involved, Mr.

Linney, but I suppose, like anything else, it takes a little getting used to. I've been doing this since I was a young girl, you see."

"Your family, they have always been farmers then, Miss Quiner?" Mr. Linney asked.

"My father was a fur trader as well as a farmer when he came west to Wisconsin," Caroline answered, "but he was a blacksmith back east, and my mother was a dressmaker in Boston."

"Boston! A wonderful city!" Mr. Linney cried, eyes lighting up. "Have you ever been there, Miss Quiner?"

Caroline shook her head. She felt she knew Boston through her mother's stories and through her grandparents' letters, but she had never seen the city with her own eyes, and wondered if she ever would.

Mr. Linney began to reminisce about Boston. "Such a cultivated, civilized place! It is where I first began to teach. Schools there are nothing like the backwoods schools here, I assure you."

Caroline caught her breath. She wondered if Mr. Linney would realize he had said something that might offend, but he did not. He continued to talk glowingly about the schools in Boston. Caroline listened, shrugging off the casual remark. She was sure Mr. Linney had not meant to criticize her personally. All he knew was that she had gone to college in Milwaukee. How could he possibly know that the rest of her schooling had been received in the "backwoods"? It did not matter anyway. Caroline was proud of her education, and she was proud of teaching at Concord School.

Mr. Linney continued his monologue about Boston and what a wonderful place it was. Caroline wanted to listen, but as her hands busily worked, she found her mind wandering. She looked up to see Eliza watching her. Eliza was sitting with her friends, but she scrunched up her nose so that Caroline knew she was deeply disappointed that it was Mr. Linney and not Charles who had claimed a seat beside her.

Caroline gave a little shake of her head and looked away. Except for the young girls making cornhusk dolls in one corner and the young boys still playing tag, most people had come to join the circle of huskers. Under the hum of conversation was the soft sound of the crisp papery husks being pulled away and the freed cobs falling into growing piles.

Caroline still did not see Charles anywhere, but when she glanced at Polly, she was amazed to see that Henry had taken the empty seat on the hay bale beside her.

Polly's face was flushed pink, and her dark eyes were sparkling in the lantern light. She and Henry were obviously having fun, racing each other to see who could husk corn the fastest.

Caroline was so deeply surprised, her hands paused for a moment and she lost the rhythm of her work. Had Henry made a point of sitting beside Polly? It was true that Henry had always seemed to take particular pleasure in playfully teasing Polly when they were younger, but Caroline had never thought much about it. Besides, Henry was just as uninterested in settling down as

Charles, determined to go off on some adventure west.

"Do you not think so, Miss Quiner?" Mr. Linney asked then, and Caroline gave a start.

With embarrassment she realized that Mr. Linney had posed a question and she had been rudely distracted.

"I am sorry, Mr. Linney, I am afraid I did not hear your question," Caroline said.

"I was just commenting on how nice it is when neighbors get together in this way to help one another," Mr. Linney replied. "Concord could never compare to a great city like Boston, of course, but it is a friendly place, don't you think so?"

"Yes, I do, Mr. Linney," Caroline was glad to be able to answer.

Just then a jolly sound was heard. It was a fiddle starting up. Charles had hopped up on a makeshift stage made of hay bales and had begun to jauntily play "The Blue-tail Fly."

Shouts of appreciation rose up among the huskers, and when Charles came to the refrain, many voices joined in to sing:

"Jimmie crack corn and I don't care,
Jimmie crack corn and I don't care,
Jimmie crack corn and I don't care,
The boss has gone away!"

When that song was done, Charles played another fast tune. The lively music seemed to make everyone work more quickly. Golden tassels and papery husks flew into the air as couples and friends began to race, trying to beat each other. Even Mr. Linney seemed to speed up a little.

As she worked, Caroline glanced at Charles now and then. His brow was knitted in concentration as he moved the bow in an impossibly quick rhythm.

"That young man certainly can play the fiddle," Mr. Linney commented. "It's rare to find such a good musician here in the backwoods."

Again the word *backwoods* pricked at Caroline's pride, but only for a brief moment. It was silly to be angry with Mr. Linney, who meant no harm, and it was certainly impossible

to stay cross when such cheerful music was being played.

Charles played "Old Dan Tucker" and "Durang's Hornpipe." He grinned and dipped and bowed as the notes flew from the strings. After a while his thick dark hair sprang up in places where even the bear grease could not hold it down. Caroline had a deep urge to go and run a hand through Charles's hair to smooth it.

"Oh, oh, oh!"

A startled cry came from somewhere close by, followed by whoops of laughter.

"Red ear! Red ear! She's got a red ear!" somebody shouted, and the whole room turned to see who had found a red ear of corn.

It was Polly! Her face was crimson. She tried to throw the red cob away as if it were a hot potato, but a group of boys—led by her own brother Jamie—swarmed up and quickly retrieved the cob and held it over her head, singing, "Red ear, red ear, Polly's got a red ear!"

The chant started among the boys but was

quickly taken up by the grown-ups, and soon the whole barn shook with the sound.

"Red ear, red ear, Polly's got a red ear!"

"Kiss him! Kiss him! Kiss him quick and don't be slow!"

Polly hid her burning face in her hands and shook her head as the chanting went on and on. Caroline imagined how she would feel to be the center of attention in such a way. She knew she would hate it, and she felt sorry for Polly's predicament.

"You know the rules. You gotta give the boy a kiss!" someone shouted.

Polly's head popped up and she leaned over, swiftly planting a kiss on Henry's cheek.

Henry's eyes opened wide, and a burst of color shot up from his neck to his hairline until he was red as a beet. He looked so stunned, Caroline found herself laughing out loud.

"That's it! That's the ticket!" voices shouted. "She got you good, Quiner! How 'bout one more kiss for luck!"

Polly hid her face in her hands again, but Caroline could see that she was smiling behind her fingers and her shoulders were shaking with laughter.

The ribbing looked as if it would never end, but then the fiddle rose up above all the commotion. The song was "Billy Boy," and voices began to sing:

> *"Oh, where have you been, Billy Boy, Billy*
> *Boy?*
> *Oh, where have you been, Charming Billy?*
> *I have gone to seek a wife; she's the joy*
> *of my life.*
> *But she's a young thing, and cannot leave*
> *her mother."*

When the song was over, Joseph and his friends came over to joke with Henry. Henry pushed them away, scowling, but Caroline noticed that when he glanced back at Polly, he seemed strangely sober. Polly herself was keeping her eyes down, watching her hands, but she wore a little smile on her still-blushing face.

Dance All Night

With all the lively music and singing and laughter, the work was quickly done. Soon the great mountain of corn had been replaced by hills of bare shucked ears. The barn floor was littered with dry husks.

Mr. Spivey announced that it was time to eat, and a great shout rose up from the workers.

Caroline stood and brushed the dust and golden tassels from her skirt. She was very glad she had made it through the husking without finding a red ear herself.

"Shall I escort you to the table, Miss Quiner?" Mr. Linney asked.

"Do not trouble yourself, Mr. Linney," Caroline said kindly. She did not want to be rude, but she wanted to gently nip in the bud any real interest Mr. Linney might have in her. "I must go find my sisters."

If Mr. Linney was disappointed, he did not show it. He bowed again and said, "Very well, Miss Quiner. Thank you for your company. I understand there will be music later, and I do hope you will save one dance for me."

"I would be delighted, Mr. Linney," Caroline answered.

After he had turned away, Caroline gave a little inward sigh of relief and moved to find her sisters in the crowd, but someone grabbed her by the arm. It was Polly.

"Oh, Caroline! Can you believe I got a red ear! I was never so embarrassed in my whole life!" she whispered.

"Well, at least it was Henry and not some stranger," Caroline whispered back.

"Yes, at least it was Henry," Polly said in a

subdued voice, and Caroline saw that Polly was gazing off to one side with a strangely serene expression on her lovely face. Then her eyes focused and she whispered, "Oh, Caroline, I did feel sorry for you sitting next to Mr. Linney. Was it awful? Do you think he wants to court you?"

"No, it wasn't awful," Caroline whispered back. "He is quite nice, really. I think he's just a little lonely and out of place here. He wanted to talk about teaching and give me advice if I needed it."

"I hope you told him that you are doing fine without his old advice," Polly said indignantly.

"Of course I said no such thing, Polly Ingalls." Caroline laughed. "I could always use advice from someone more experienced."

Polly shook her head. "I think you are the best teacher we've ever had, and not because you are my friend, but because it is true."

"Thank you, Polly!" Caroline cried.

At the food table Caroline tried to put a little bit of everything on her tin plate; then she and Polly went to join Martha and Charlie and Eliza and Margaret and Docia where they sat on a cluster of hay bales. Joseph and Henry and Thomas came up with their plates piled high. Caroline wondered where Charles might be, then saw him sitting with his parents, playing with baby Lansford.

All through the meal Caroline noticed Henry and Polly exchanging quick glances, but they were both quiet and did not laugh and joke with the rest as much. At one point Polly leaned in to Caroline and whispered, "I don't think you have to be worried about Mr. Linney being lonely now!"

Caroline looked to where Polly was nodding. Mr. Linney and Maddy were sitting alone together! Mr. Linney seemed to be talking in a monologue, as he had done with Caroline, but Maddy appeared to be listening intently. Caroline was glad he had found a more attentive audience than herself.

After all had eaten their fill, the young women helped clear the dishes and pack them away while the young men moved hay bales to make an area big enough for dancing.

"We'd best be quick—otherwise we'll be snowed in, and then we'd have to dance all night long!" somebody said.

"I wouldn't mind!" somebody else replied.

Caroline gasped. How could she have forgotten all about the weather and Pa's warning? She turned to look for her brothers, but it was Charles she found, standing before her. He had smoothed down his hair again, and his eyes were smiling, but when he saw the worry on her face, his expression changed instantly.

"Is something wrong, Caroline?" he asked.

"Oh, I was just wondering if it had started to snow yet," Caroline said fretfully. "Pa told us it might and that we should head home at the first hint of bad weather."

"Let's go take a look, shall we?" Charles said, and Caroline followed him across the room.

The great barn doors had been opened a foot, and some people had gathered about, looking out at the night.

Right away, Caroline noticed that the night air did not have the same bite to it and the stars and moon had disappeared into an inky blackness. She did not think these were good signs. If it was warming up a bit and clouding over, it could mean snow.

"Pa warned us there might be a bad snow-storm," she said.

Mr. Ingalls had joined the little group, and he nodded thoughtfully.

"I think I'll go ahead and take Mrs. Ingalls and the young'uns home. I'm too old to dance anyway, and I always trust what Frederick says about the weather." Mr. Ingalls gave Caroline a nod and went to find his wife.

Caroline's stomach twisted into a nervous knot. Once more she turned to look for Joseph and Henry and Thomas.

"Caroline Quiner, you're certainly not too old to dance, and it isn't snowing yet," Charles said.

Caroline turned back to find him gazing at her.

"I was hoping you might save a dance for me," he added softly.

Caroline knew the color was rising in her cheeks. "But you are the fiddler, Charles Ingalls!" she protested, though she couldn't help but smile as she said it. "Who would play for you?"

"We'll see," Charles answered with a wink. Then he turned on his heel and strode jauntily through the crowd. Taking up his fiddle, he leaped onto a hay bale and immediately launched into a quick tune. "Here we go!" he shouted over the lively notes. "Find a partner, boys, now don't be slow!"

Instantly the room broke off into couples. Caroline saw that Henry had taken Polly by the hand, and Charlie and Martha were already starting to jig.

"Would you be so kind as to give me the honor of this dance, Miss Quiner?" Joseph asked Caroline, giving a little mock bow.

"Why, I would be happy to, Mr. Quiner," Caroline playfully answered, following her brother to the line of dancers.

"Bow to your partners, do-si-do! Swing 'em 'round now, don't be slow," Charles's voice called.

Caroline curtsied to Joseph and he bowed back, and then they circled each other back to back. All down the line the other dancers did the same. The cornhusks scattered and flew across the barn floor as skirts swirled and boots stomped.

"Now you turn left and then you turn right! Spin that gal with all your might!"

Charles sang out the calls and the couples merrily obeyed. Caroline let her tangled thoughts slip away in the happy rhythm of the dance. Every face she passed was smiling and carefree, and she wanted to be the same.

When one song ended, the fiddle swung seamlessly into another. Charles played "Turkey in the Straw" and then "Divide the Ring":

"First couple balance and first couple sing!
Down the center and divide the ring!"

After dancing with Joseph through the first few songs, Caroline danced with Thomas and then Mr. Kellogg and then Mr. Spivey and then with two bachelors she did not know. Mr. Linney came to ask her next, but they danced only one dance together. He seemed eager to get back to Maddy's side.

When Henry came to claim her, Caroline teased him. "I am surprised you want to jig with your own sister! Polly is certainly a better dancer than I am."

Henry grinned his donkey grin. "I reckon a fella's got to let a girl catch her breath."

As the evening wore on, Caroline did not forget that Charles had asked her to save a dance for him. She did not really think he would be able to dance with her, but for some reason, knowing that he wanted to made her feel light on her feet. Twice as she twirled about the room, she glanced up to find his eyes watching her, and this made her heart seem to beat faster.

At last she decided to take a rest. She was just finishing a cup of the apple cider Mr.

Spivey had brought out for the dancers when she heard the fiddle pause in its playing, and she guessed that Charles was taking a rest as well. Right away the music started up again, however; but it sounded different somehow, as if Charles were suddenly less sure of the notes.

She turned toward the hay-bale stage and saw that it was not Charles playing the fiddle at all. It was Mr. Fleming!

Then Charles himself was standing before her, eyes full of mischief.

"May I have this dance, Caroline?" he asked, and gave a little bow.

Caroline's heart seemed to stop beating altogether. The whole room of dancers had turned to watch Charles after he had given up his post, and now they were all waiting to see what Caroline would do. It was a little like being the one with the red ear. A part of her wanted to turn and hide behind a hay bale, but a bigger part yearned to dance with Charles.

"Yes, Charles," Caroline said, raising her chin in the air. She would not let anyone know how nervous she felt. "You may have this dance."

She took his hand and followed him to the middle of the dance floor. There was some laughter and clapping, but Caroline ignored it. She concentrated on keeping her head high as the dance began.

The song was "Buffalo Gals," and the playing was not as smooth as when Charles played, but it was a lively tune nonetheless, one of Caroline's favorites.

> *"Oh, you Buffalo gals!*
> *Will you come out tonight?*
> *Will you come out tonight?*
> *Will you come out tonight?*
> *Buffalo gals!*
> *Will you come out tonight,*
> *To dance by the light of the moon?"*

For a brief moment the lyrics made Caroline think of the night sky, and she wondered whether or not it had started to snow. But as Charles dipped and twirled her about the room, serious thoughts slipped away.

"I told you I'd find a way to dance with you, and by George, I did," Charles said, smiling down at her.

Caroline couldn't help but smile back. "I did not know Mr. Fleming could play," she said.

"Well, I thought he was pretty musical, what with playing the fife and all, so I asked him and he said he could play a song or two," Charles answered.

After "Buffalo Gals," Mr. Fleming slowed the tempo down and began a waltz. Charles matched his step perfectly to the music, and Caroline daintily followed his lead. They swept about the room in great circles. The other dancers became a blur, and Caroline felt a little breathless.

After the waltz, Mr. Fleming launched into another popular song. Again his thin voice sang the melody:

> *"I dream of Jeanie with the light brown hair,*
> *Floating, like a vapor, on the soft summer*
> *air."*

Caroline felt like a vapor herself, floating, floating, in dozy circles. Around and around she went, whirling but steady in Charles's strong arms. It was a lovely sensation of being airborne yet grounded, and she did not want it to end. She glanced tentatively up at Charles's face and found that he was watching her again.

As the song was coming to an end, a great gust of wind suddenly shook the barn to its very foundation.

"Jumping Jehosophat! Look at the snow!" a voice shouted.

"Snow!" Caroline whispered. She and Charles exchanged a worried glance. Together they hurried to the barn door, where everyone was gathering.

Mr. Spivey was sliding the door open to reveal the scene outside. Caroline gasped, and Charles let out a low whistle. The ground was already covered by several inches of snow, and the night sky was a blur of white.

"How did it come up so fast?" a voice asked.

"I guess we were too busy to notice," another voice replied.

"Your pa was right, Caroline," Charles said, looking grim.

"He usually is," Caroline said. "We should have listened to him and gone home before the snow set in."

"It's my fault!" Charles exclaimed. "I should not have persuaded you to stay."

"It's nobody's fault," Caroline said matter-of-factly, and then she added in a very quiet voice, "I wanted to stay."

Joseph and Henry had joined the group, and Caroline turned to them. "We should go now," she said.

Joseph did not answer right away. He and Henry were watching the snow.

"Think we should risk it?" Henry asked.

"I don't know," Joseph said. "We'd have to take the wheels off the wagon to make a sled. The oxen could probably do it, but it would be slow going."

"Looks like a bad snowstorm to me," Charles spoke up. "We might get caught halfway home and then get turned around in the snow. I've heard of men who have frozen to death not five feet from their doorstep."

Caroline's stomach twisted into a knot of fear. She knew Charles spoke the truth. Last year a snowstorm had blown up out of nowhere. Two brothers had died halfway to their cabin on their way from town.

"Maybe if we all stick together . . ." Henry began, but Charles shook his head.

"I would risk it myself, but not with my sisters and younger brothers in tow," he said. "Maybe Mr. Spivey will let us all bed down here for the night."

"Of course, of course!" Mr. Spivey spoke up then. "I urge you all to stay. We can make it quite comfortable for the ladies, I assure you. It will be warm in the barn, and at least all of you will be safe."

"What do you think?" Charles asked. He looked first at Joseph and Henry, then his gaze settled on Caroline.

Caroline turned to watch the snow again. An image of Mother's worried face came to her.

She knew that Mother would stay up all night, waiting and praying for their safe return, and this certain knowledge made Caroline's stomach churn. How could she have let herself be so swept away with the dancing that she had not heeded Pa's warning?

Feeling guilty and angry with herself would not help the situation now. A decision had to be made right away, and Charles was looking at her as if the decision rested upon her shoulders alone.

"I think we should stay," Caroline said in a firm voice.

"Now we can dance all night!" Henry joked.

But Caroline did not smile. Gazing out upon the snow falling heavily from the sky, she did not feel much like dancing anymore.

Snowed In

For the next hour everyone was busy getting ready for the long night ahead. The men went to fetch blankets and quilts from the Spiveys' house and tend to the animals. The horses were brought into the back room of the large barn. The oxen were left outside but tied against the west wall to keep them out of the worst of the wind and drifting snow.

When the men came back inside, it looked as though they had dressed in white from head to toe.

Snowed In

"It's really coming down," Charles said, shaking the snow from his coat and trousers and hat. "You can hardly see your own hand in front of your face."

Caroline kept herself busy by helping tear apart hay bales and spread the quilts over the tops to make soft beds. At least they would be comfortable and safe. As she worked, she tried not to think of Mother standing at the window, peering out into the snowy night. If only she had been more prudent, and watched the weather instead of frivolously dancing away the hours! But she knew there was no use in crying over spilled milk, as Mother liked to say.

"What should we do now?" someone asked when the animals had been seen to and the beds made.

"It's early yet!"

"Let's keep dancing!"

"How about it, Ingalls?"

They all looked to Charles. He shrugged his shoulders. "I don't mind playing if that's what folks want."

And so it was decided that the dancing would go on. Charles took his place again and began to play.

Caroline did not really feel like dancing anymore, but it was hard to say no when Joseph asked her after the first few songs had played. The music was so jolly, it was hard to keep still. And it was true that there was not much to do now that they were snowed in. They could not get home, after all, and Caroline had not brought any sewing or knitting to do. She noticed that it was mostly young couples and boys and girls who had stayed. Many of the older couples, like the Kelloggs, had had the foresight to go home before the snow began.

Outside, the storm raged. The wind rattled the great doors and tried to drown out the fiddle with its whining. It was a strange feeling to be dancing merrily inside the barn while just beyond the plank walls the storm wind blew.

Some said they wanted to dance all night, but Caroline intended to sleep. They would need to get up early if they ever wanted to dig themselves out of the snow and get home.

When she grew tired, she went to find a place in the hay, and Martha followed her. One by one the couples parted; the men went to one side of the barn and the women went to the other. Mr. Spivey dimmed the lanterns, though he left the stove going, and it filled the barn with a soft glow.

Caroline and her sisters and friends settled close to one another on the beds of hay. Some dozed off right away, but others chatted quietly.

Eliza snuggled close to Caroline's side. "You looked so pretty dancing with Charles," she whispered. "Was it fun?"

"Yes, it was," Caroline answered, though she felt another pang of guilt as she said it. It had been the lure of dancing with Charles that had caused her to lose track of her promise to Mother and Pa to come home before the bad weather started. Then she thought of another promise she had nearly forgotten. She had told Lottie she would bring her a cornhusk doll.

Caroline felt around the floor for some husks and quickly began to twist and knot them into a head and body and skirt. As she worked in the dim light, she listened to the wind moan and howl and beat against the barn. The sound made her shiver and yearn to be home in her own bed.

Presently another sound started up over the storm. It was Charles's fiddle, playing a tune that was familiar though Caroline could not recall exactly when and where she had heard it. His deep voice turned lilting, like a Scottish brogue, and he crooned softly:

"My heart is sair, I dare na tell,
My heart is sair for Somebody;
I could wake a winter-night,
For the sake o' Somebody.—

"Ye Powers that smile on virtuous love,
O, sweetly smile on Somebody!
Frae ilka danger keep her free,
And send me safe my Somebody.—"

It was a haunting melody, and the lyrics made her heart heavy with longing and sadness. How strange that a mere song could affect her so deeply!

> *"Ohon! for Somebody!*
> *Oh-hey! for Somebody!*
> *I could range the warld round,*
> *For the sake o' Somebody.—"*

Charles's deep baritone grew plaintive as he sang the song through to its melancholy end. A hush fell over the room.

After a few quiet moments Charles began to play again. This time the song was a lullaby, soft and sweet.

Caroline finished the cornhusk doll and tucked it inside her coat pocket. Then she lay back and closed her eyes, settling herself deeper into the hay. She listened to the fiddle as it rose up over the howl of the wind. The music made her feel quiet and peaceful, and in a very short time she drifted off into sleep.

Her dreams that night were full of motion.

One minute she was dancing, the next she was riding in a buggy speeding down a winding road, rushing toward home. A man was in the seat beside her, driving the team of horses, urging them to go faster and faster. Even though she could not see the driver's face, she felt a deep gladness to be at his side.

Next she was in a vast, densely wooded wilderness. Again someone was with her, walking just ahead on the path, and she thought it was Father, but she could not see through the trees and she could not catch up to him no matter how hard she tried. She wanted to call for him, but no sound came out of her mouth. She began to run, but the figure disappeared around a bend, and then she was all alone.

She awoke with a start and did not know where she was at first. Then she saw the rafters above her and felt the hay at her back, and she remembered. She was in Mr. Spivey's barn.

Pale morning light trickled in between the wide wooden planks of the barn walls. The wind had stopped its terrible moaning, and all was quiet. Martha and Eliza were breathing deeply beside her, and she could hear the horses snorting and stomping their hooves in the back of the barn.

Caroline lay still for a few moments more. When she heard the men stirring on the other side of the room, she sat up, plucking the hay from her hair and smoothing her bun as best she could. Then she stood and brushed off her coat and skirt, hoping she did not look too rumpled. Gently she shook her sisters awake. Polly and Docia and the other girls and women were just starting to open their eyes, blinking sleepily.

On the other side of the barn the men were sliding the barn door open.

"Will you look at that!" one of them said.

When Caroline glimpsed the outside, she caught her breath. It was as if a giant had laid a heavy white blanket over everything. The snow was easily four feet deep—and even higher in the places where it had drifted against trees and outbuildings.

"What about the oxen?" Caroline anxiously

asked her brothers. "Are they buried?"

"No," Joseph answered. "We all took turns going out to check on them during the night, so there are paths cleared for them already. But the wagons are another story."

"What can we do?" Polly asked. She and Docia and Martha and Eliza had come up beside Caroline.

"Not much for you to do right now until we get the paths cleared," Henry said.

The men went to get shovels and picks and headed out into the snow. Mr. Spivey came in carrying baskets of food.

"There's not much, I'm afraid," he said as he brought out loaves of bread, a tin of Swedish crackers, some cheese, salt pork, and apples.

"It's plenty, Mr. Spivey—thank you so much," Caroline spoke up. "You did not expect us for breakfast when we came for a cornhusking!"

"No, I certainly did not," Mr. Spivey said, chuckling. "But I'm just glad everyone's safe this morning."

Mr. Spivey went off to help the men, and Caroline and the other young women set about dividing up the food and making sandwiches for everyone to eat.

"I bet Mrs. Spivey was not happy about giving us even this much to eat for breakfast!" Martha whispered in Caroline's ear.

The men stopped to eat the sandwiches and the apples. Then they went back to shoveling snow. It took over an hour to dig the paths and get the oxen and wagons ready to go through the snow.

"We took the wheels off the wagon to use as a sled. But even so, we'll have to help the oxen cut a path home through the woods. The drifts will be pretty high," Joseph said. "It will be slow going."

"Let's stick together in a wagon train," Charles suggested. "That way the second wagon will have an easier time. And we'll all be together to help with the digging."

"Good idea," Henry said.

"What about your horse and buggy?" Martha asked Charlie.

"Mr. Spivey said he'd keep 'em for a spell," Charlie answered. "The oxen will do better through the snow. And the most important thing right now is getting you gals home."

"Your ma and pa will be worried too," Martha said.

"They'll figure I stayed with you folks to wait out the weather," Charlie replied confidently.

Caroline put on her coat and muffler and followed the others outside into the snowy world. It was not as cold as the night before, but it was blindingly bright as she came out of the barn. The snow crunched underfoot. When Martha strayed a little from the path the men had dug, she sank in over her knees and Caroline had to help pull her out.

Jamie and Hiram Ingalls and Thomas started a snowball fight with Docia and Eliza, but Charles put an end to the fun by gruffly saying, "No time for games now."

Everyone piled into the wagons that had been made into sleds. Some people only had a short distance to go to get to their homes, but others had much farther. It was easily more than six miles back through the woods to the Ingallses' cabin and about another mile to Mother and Pa. Caroline thought of how long the journey had seemed the night before in the cold dark. It would seem even longer now with four feet of snow covering the ground.

"Good-bye! Good-bye!" voices called out as folks parted and went their separate ways.

"Good luck! God be with you!" Mr. Spivey cried, waving from his door.

Henry helped Caroline and Martha and Eliza up into the wagon, and they filed in behind the Ingallses' wagon. Thomas sat in the front, driving the team of oxen, while Joseph and Henry and Charlie walked with the shovels borrowed from Mr. Spivey.

Without wheels, the wagon floated upon the snow behind the oxen, and it seemed to Caroline that they were in a small boat sailing over a strange white sea. As they entered the woods, the bushes and low trees were covered in snow and looked like fantastical white creatures rising up from the waves.

Once they were deeper into the woods, the going was slow, just as Joseph had predicted. The oxen did the best they could, their great legs plodding through the heavy snow. But in some places the drifts were so deep, the oxen sank up to their withers and could not budge. Then the boys had to dig them out.

As the wagon train of two pushed slowly on, Caroline wished there were something more she could do besides simply sitting while the men worked so hard. But she knew she was not strong enough to dig out the oxen, and her skirt and petticoats would soon grow wet and heavy against her legs if she tried to walk in the deep drifts.

An hour passed and they were not even halfway home. Then the sun suddenly disappeared behind a wall of gray clouds and the woods darkened all around them.

"It feels like snow again," Caroline said to Martha in a low voice.

"I'm afraid you're right," Martha answered.

"It won't snow again!" Eliza cried. "How could it?"

But Caroline looked at Charles and her brothers up ahead. They had stopped to watch the sky, and she knew they were thinking the same thing.

Now the boys tried to pick up the pace, but the oxen could not go very far without getting completely stuck in the high drifts. In a little while Caroline felt the first soft flakes brush against her cheek, and then the air became a flurry of white.

"Do you think Pa will come looking for us?" Eliza asked fretfully.

"Yes, I am sure he will," Caroline answered.

"Then his legs will ache even more," Eliza wailed, "and it will be all our fault."

Caroline did not say anything right away. It was terrible to think of Pa setting out into the snow, trying to dig his way through despite the pain in his legs.

"Perhaps it is just a little snow," Caroline said at last, trying to sound more hopeful than she felt.

But it was not a little snow. The flurries multiplied until the air was thick with white flakes and it was difficult to see, as if a veil had fallen over everything.

The oxen pushed onward, but it took longer and longer to dig them out of the deepening drifts. Caroline tried to gauge how far they had come, but it was hard to tell with so much snow covering the trees.

The wind began to pick up, blowing in fierce gusts. It whistled sharply through the trees and made the snow feel like stinging nettles against any bare skin.

Eliza let out a little whimper, and Caroline reached out to try to wrap one of the blankets more tightly about her sister's body. Then she put an arm around Eliza and hugged her close.

"It will be all right," Caroline said over the roar of the wind. "We will be home soon."

Martha moved to sit closer to Eliza on the other side, so they were a tight little group to combat the cold. Caroline closed her eyes against the blinding snow. She felt the wagon start and stop, start and stop. After a while she was not sure how much time had passed.

When she squinted her eyes open again, it seemed to her that they had been in the woods a very long time. She could just make out Charles tromping back through the snow to speak to Joseph. The boys nodded, and then Joseph came up beside her.

"The Ingallses' place is closer. We're going to head there and wait out the storm."

Caroline nodded. She could not speak. Her teeth were chattering now, and she could feel Eliza shivering beside her. She thought of Mother and Pa and how worried they would be. But Charles was right. It was best to seek shelter as soon as possible in case the storm grew even worse.

After a time, as they made their slow way through the woods, Caroline began to grow sleepy. Rocking back and forth with the motion of the wagon, she felt herself giving in to the feeling. How nice it would be to simply doze off for a moment—

"Eliza! Martha!" she cried, making herself sit bolt upright. Suddenly she had remembered something Pa had once told her. When caught out in a storm, it was important never to fall asleep. A person could freeze to death that way. "Eliza! Martha!" she called again more loudly.

"Yes, Caroline," Martha said, and then Eliza said, "What is it?"

"We must stay awake!" Caroline waited for a response but didn't hear any. She pushed her muffler down away from her face. The snow was so heavy, it was hard to see. She bumped Eliza and then leaned over and shook Martha.

"All right, all right!" Martha said.

"I'm awake," said Eliza.

"Let us keep talking," Caroline suggested. Then she yelled to Joseph until he came back to see what she wanted. "Tell Polly to keep talking. Tell them not to fall asleep."

Joseph nodded and headed back toward the front of the wagon. Then Caroline said, "Let us recite something together—the Lord's Prayer." She began to say the words, but her sisters did not join in right away, so she yelled, "Let us recite!"

"Yes, Miss Quiner," Martha said, and Eliza managed a chuckle.

Caroline began to recite the prayer, and her sisters' voices soon joined in: "Our Father who art in heaven, hallowed be thy name. Thy kingdom come, thy will be done, on earth, as it is in heaven. . . ."

When they came to the end of the prayer, Caroline's thoughts were sluggish, but she made herself recite a Bible verse, and after a moment her sisters joined in. She was not sure how many verses they had said when she heard a shout and saw a light through the veil of snow.

"We made it!" she cried. "We're safe!"

The wagon stopped and the door to the Ingallses' cabin flew open. Before Caroline knew what was happening, she was being lifted out of the wagon by Joseph and carried into the warmth.

Safe and Sound

"Is this the way you young men court a girl nowadays—freeze her to death?" Mr. Ingalls cried once they were all seated around the roaring fire in the Ingallses' cozy kitchen, hot mugs of tea in their hands.

Caroline tried to smile. She knew Mr. Ingalls was just making a joke. But her face still felt stiff from the cold. At least her toes and fingers had stopped their painful tingling and the feeling had returned to them. Mrs. Ingalls had made the girls and boys all change out of their wet clothes. Caroline was wearing one of Polly's wool dresses and a woolen shawl.

"Goodness gracious, why didn't you come home before the snow began?" Mrs. Ingalls demanded as she refilled the mugs of tea.

"The snow came up so fast, ma'am," Henry said.

"Caroline tried to warn us," Charles spoke up.

"And why didn't you listen to her?" Mrs. Ingalls wanted to know.

"It was Pa we should have listened to," Caroline said then. She did not want Mrs. Ingalls scolding the rest when she was just as much to blame.

"I wish we could send word to your parents that you are safe, but we can't risk it now," Mr. Ingalls said, glancing toward the window.

Outside, the wind continued to blow fiercely and the snow was falling fast.

"We'll start home as soon as we're able. Surely this storm will let up!" said Joseph. "I've never seen a snowstorm this early before."

"Well, we shall make the best of it," Mrs.

Ingalls said brightly. "I always like to have you folks to visit, of course. I just wish it weren't on account of a storm!"

Caroline felt the same way. She always enjoyed visiting the Ingallses. They were generous hosts, and their log cabin was especially homey, with colorful rag rugs covering the wide plank floors and red-and-white-checked curtains at the windows. The rooms always smelled of apples and cloves and cinnamon. At this time of year braids of onions hung from the rafters, and every corner held pyramids of orange pumpkins and golden squash.

"I know you must be hungry!" Mrs. Ingalls continued. "Did you eat anything at all this morning?"

"Not very much!" Jamie said.

"Mrs. Spivey did not want to feed us, the stingy old thing!" Docia mumbled.

"Laura Ladocia!" Mrs. Ingalls cried, aghast. "Mind your manners!"

Mrs. Ingalls set about making them dinner, and Caroline was glad to be able to help. She wanted to keep busy so that she would not have to dwell on thoughts of Mother and Pa and how worried they would be. So she peeled and cut potatoes and set them in the pan to fry while Mrs. Ingalls brought out strips of dried venison to fry up as well.

After the table had been set, everyone crowded together on the long benches. Mr. Ingalls gave thanks for keeping them all safe in the storm, and said a prayer for the unfortunate souls who might still be out in the cold.

Caroline's thoughts flew to Maddy and Mr. Linney and the others who had set off for town. They had had a shorter distance to travel. Surely they had made it home before the storm had hit again. Then she thought of Pa. She hoped with all her might that he had not gone too far into the woods trying to find them.

After all the good food was eaten, Caroline helped clear the table. She wiped the dishes and swept around the table, even though Mrs. Ingalls told her not to trouble herself. When

Baby Lansford, sleeping in his cradle near the fire, began to fuss, she picked him up, since she was the closest, and soothed him. He settled happily in her arms. She walked him across the room to the window to gaze outside.

It was dark, even though it was afternoon. The wind howled under the eaves of the cabin, and the air was full of snow.

"Your folks will most likely guess you spent the night with the Spiveys, and that you stopped again here to wait out the storm," Charles said, coming up beside her.

"I hope so," Caroline replied.

Just then Baby Lansford began to fuss again, reaching out his chubby hands for Charles.

"Come here, little man," Charles said, chuckling. He took the baby and swung him high into the air. Baby Lansford cooed with delight.

Mrs. Ingalls made more hot tea and brought out the cookies she had baked that morning. They all settled in around the fire again, and Caroline and Martha sat down to help Polly and Lydia with the quilt they were making. The boys played checkers while the young men whittled and talked politics with Mr. Ingalls, who always made a point of reading the most recent newspapers from the east when they arrived at Mr. Jayson's store.

"What a terrible mess this bank business has caused in this great country!" Mr. Ingalls said.

Caroline knew that the "bank business" was what had happened to banks back east. A number of banks in New York City had shut down completely, and people had lost all their money. It was causing a panic, and the panic was spreading across the country. Caroline did not really understand. There were no banks in Concord. But the panic was affecting everything, even the price of wheat.

"I've never trusted banks," Mr. Ingalls continued. "Land is the best way to invest your money—I've always thought so."

"Pa thinks the same way," Joseph said.

"And all that gold they were trying to bring from California to bail out the banks!" Mr.

Ingalls continued. "Gone! All gone!"

"Thirty thousand pounds of gold!" Henry cried, eyes lighting up. "Can you imagine that much gold all together!"

"The newspapers say the ship went down off the coast of South Carolina," Charles said, shaking his head. "Sank like a stone with all that gold, it did!"

"Maybe if a body could dive deep enough . . ." Henry said thoughtfully.

"It's at the bottom of the sea, my boy." Mr. Ingalls laughed. "The fish will divide up the wealth now!"

Soon the younger children grew restless from being inside for so long, and Charles went to get his fiddle. He gathered Ruby and George and Baby Lansford together on the floor in front of him and played "Pop! Goes the Weasel." Ruby and George watched and said "Pop!" each time Charles's thumb popped one of the fiddle strings. Charles's eyebrows flew up into a surprised expression each time his thumb went *pop!* and Ruby and George giggled until they could hardly stand.

The giggling was infectious, and Caroline couldn't help but laugh along with them.

At last the snow stopped falling and the wind settled. Henry and Joseph were anxious to get going, and so was Caroline, but Mr. Ingalls wondered if they shouldn't wait till morning.

"It's only a mile as the crow flies, of course, but the snow is mighty deep," he said. "It might take a couple of hours to get to your place."

Caroline glanced from Henry to Joseph to Charlie. "If you think we can make it, I would rather start now," she said. "We've worried Mother enough already."

"You'll make it, I promise," Charles spoke up then. "Jamie and I will come along to help."

Then all changed back into their own clothes, which were dry by now, and the boys went out to get the sled and oxen ready. Mrs. Ingalls already had potatoes warming in the stove. Now she gave them to the girls to put inside their pockets. Then she hugged Caroline and Martha and Eliza in turn.

"It's always a pleasure to see you girls," she said. "I am glad we got a chance to visit even though it was not under the best of circumstances."

"So are we," Caroline answered. "Thank you so much for everything, Mrs. Ingalls."

Outside, the sun had come out just in time to go down. The snow looked beautiful in the pinkish light. It was strange to think that something so lovely could be dangerous as well.

Charles helped Caroline and her sisters up into the wagon. In a few moments, they were deep in the darkening woods. Again they had to stop every few feet to dig the oxen out of the drifts, but once they got to the river, they were able to glide over the frozen water until they were nearly home.

When they finally reached the clearing, the moon was a sliver in the sky. The door of the house swung open, and Mother and Pa and Lottie appeared. Mother rushed out through the snow to meet the sled.

"Oh, thank goodness!" she cried.

Caroline and her sisters jumped down, and

Mother hugged them fiercely to her.

"I was so worried!" she whispered. Then her tone grew sharp. "Oh, why didn't you come home early like your pa told you to!"

Caroline felt tears sting her eyes. "We are so sorry, Mother," she and Martha and Eliza cried together.

Mother turned to Henry and Joseph and said in the same sharp voice, "You two should have known better than to keep your sisters and brother out all night long! And Charlie Carpenter, I would have thought you had more sense!"

The young men all hung their heads. "Sorry, ma'am," they murmured.

"It is my fault," Charles said, coming forward. "I was playing the fiddle and having such fun, I persuaded them to stay so that I'd have an audience. I am truly sorry that I caused you all that worry, ma'am."

Mother turned to study Charles, and her green eyes were fierce in the fading light. Caroline held her breath, wondering what Mother would say, but after a moment her face softened a bit. "Well, all's well that ends well, I suppose. Isn't that what Mr. Shakespeare wrote in one of his plays, Caroline?" Mother asked, and Caroline nodded, letting out a silent sigh of relief.

"I have supper warming on the stove," Mother continued. "I was hoping against hope you would make it home tonight." She nodded to Charles and Jamie. "You boys are welcome to join us."

"Thank you, ma'am, but we'd best get home in case of more snow. We've already made a path between our houses, and I wouldn't want to have to do the work again," Charles said. "I just wanted to make sure everyone was safe and where they should be."

"Thank you," Mother said, and Caroline was glad she did not seem so fierce anymore.

"I wish you all a good evening," Charles said, tipping his hat. Then he and Jamie set off for home.

The boys went to the barn with the wagon and oxen while Caroline and her sisters hurried inside. Caroline had never been so glad to be home. She hugged Mother again, and then she hugged Pa and held out the salve Mrs. Ingalls had made.

"Mrs. Ingalls gave us this for your legs," Caroline said. "We were worried that you would come looking for us, and then your legs would be worse. Are they?"

Pa shook his head. "I didn't get too far, and I turned back when the snow started up again. My legs aren't too bad, but I am always glad for Mrs. Ingalls's salve."

"Did you bring me a cornhusk dolly?" Lottie asked when Caroline came to give her a hug.

"Of course I did!" Caroline carefully brought the doll out of her coat pocket. The skirt was a little bent, but Caroline smoothed it out.

Lottie's blue eyes lit up as she fingered the delicate cornhusks twisted and knotted together.

"Oh, thank you, thank you!" Lottie cried, holding the doll against her chest.

After they were all seated for supper,

Joseph explained everything that had happened.

"I told Charlotte that Spivey would have had you stay if you hadn't left in time," Pa said.

"And you were right, as usual, Frederick," Mother said. "Still, I would have thought my children, who are nearly grown now, would have known better than to stay when a storm was brewing."

"I reckon the fiddle playing must have been quite a draw," Pa said, raising an eyebrow.

"The dancing was wonderful!" Eliza breathed. "Henry danced with Polly all night long, and Caroline danced with Charles."

Caroline felt her cheeks grow warm. She kept her eyes on her plate, but she nudged Eliza under the table with her foot.

"I thought Charles was the one playing the fiddle," Pa said.

"He was, but then he stopped and asked Mr. Fleming to play so that he could dance with Caroline," Eliza continued, completely ignoring Caroline's light kicks.

"And Henry got kissed!" Thomas exclaimed, letting out a loud guffaw.

"Did he now?" Pa asked in surprise. "And who was the brave lady who gave our Henry a kiss?"

"Polly!" Eliza said, giggling.

Caroline glanced up to see Henry concentrating hard on his plate, his face beet red just as it had been at the husking.

"So that's why you didn't come home," Pa said, chuckling. "You were busy kissing and dancing all night long."

"Ugh! I didn't do any kissing or dancing!" Thomas cried indignantly. "It was all pretty silly if you ask me!"

"I'm sure it was," Pa said.

Now Caroline waited for Mother to scold them again for being so foolish. But all she said was "I am glad you had a good time, but most of all I am glad you are home safe. Next time, however, I would like you to heed your pa's warning. If he thinks you should come home early, you must do so!"

"Yes, ma'am," they all answered together.

There was a moment of sober silence, and then Lottie asked, "Why did Polly kiss Henry?"

Pa laughed loudly and everyone joined in, even Henry.

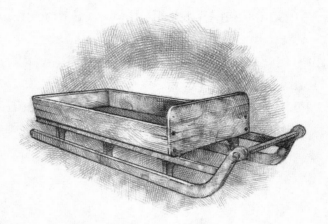

Courting Time

At school on Monday, Caroline was
relieved to learn that everyone had
reached home safely despite the
second storm. For a while the cornhusking
was the talk of the town, and Caroline could
not go anywhere without folks asking if she
was one of those who had been caught in the
barn.

At first Caroline worried about the impro-
priety, as the schoolteacher, of having been
stranded overnight at a dance. But no one
remarked upon it, and Mr. Kellogg, as head of

the school board, never chided her. When she saw him in town one day, he simply inquired how long it had taken them to get home on Saturday and said how thankful he was that no one from Concord had been lost in the snowstorm.

Soon Caroline realized that the cornhusking had done more than supply gossip for the town. It had forged a kind of bond among the young people who had been together at Mr. Spivey's. The first Saturday after the husking weekend Caroline went ice-skating on the mill pond with Polly and Maddy and some of the other girls. They were soon joined by a group of bachelors, including Henry and Charles and Joseph and Mr. Linney. After ice-skating the friends met up with Martha and Charlie and decided to all go sledding together on Concord Hill. The next Saturday they went ice-skating again, and then sleighing.

That whole day was spent rushing up and down Main Street and along Territorial Road and back. In the middle of the afternoon, Maddy invited them all to her house for mugs of warm apple cider and popcorn balls.

"Wintertime is courting time and that's a fact," Pa said when Caroline came back that evening, her cheeks rosy from the cold and the fun. "Nothing else for these bachelors to do in the winter but look for a wife. Come spring, we'll see a lot of engagements 'round here, mark my words!"

"See, Caroline, maybe you'll be engaged just like I said," Eliza whispered.

Caroline brushed Eliza's teasing aside, as she usually did, but deep down she knew that Pa was probably right. The cornhusking had created a bond, and it had also formed couples out of old friends and acquaintances.

Ever since that Friday night, Maddy seemed to be inseparable from Mr. Linney—Cyrus, as she now called him. And Elmira talked of Jonah Crab while Lucy talked of Samuel Davies, their dance partners at the husking. Polly constantly asked Caroline questions about Henry when they were alone together.

Caroline was amazed by the changes that

had taken place in her friends, literally overnight. It seemed strange that Maddy would become so smitten with the man she had called "Skinny Linney" not so long ago. And it was a wonder to Caroline that her own brother, who had never seemed serious about anything except gold and venturing off to parts unknown, would grow so quiet at the mere mention of Polly's name.

But the most bewildering change had happened within Caroline herself. Ever since the cornhusking she found her thoughts often straying to Charles. She would recall how jauntily he had played in the barn and how he had stopped his playing to dance with her. She remembered vividly the lovely feeling of being airborne in his arms.

During school or as she went about her chores at home, Caroline was often distracted. It was the same kind of distraction Martha had always shown around Charlie Carpenter, Caroline realized with astonishment. Just a few short months before, she had considered her sister's behavior strange and foolish. And here she was, acting exactly the same way!

But she couldn't help it. She found herself looking forward to those Saturday outings, anticipating the moment when she would see Charles again. She particularly enjoyed the time they spent talking together, once the group of friends had splintered off into couples.

She and Charles talked about everything: books and history and news of the day. Caroline did not feel self-conscious when she shared her views about important issues, such as slavery. When she told him about the abolitionist meetings she had attended in Milwaukee, Charles seemed very interested.

"Slavery is a terrible thing, and it surely will drive this nation apart," he solemnly said. "I think we may be headed to war."

Caroline had often heard such talk, especially at her uncle's printing shop. Still, she was not sure she believed it. "We are all neighbors in this great country. It seems impossible that one neighbor would take up the sword against another," she said.

"But look what's happened in Kansas—Bloody Kansas, as you said!" Charles cried. "Towns are divided on the slavery issue. Neighbors are killing neighbors. A great deal of blood has already been spilled over whether one man can own another."

"I suppose you are right," Caroline said, sighing. "I cannot help but believe, however, that common sense will prevail, and our leaders will put things right somehow."

"I am not sure how much common sense our politicians in Washington have! But I do hope you are the one who is right, and things turn out for the best," Charles said.

Even though she was younger than Charles by several years, she felt that he respected her opinion. Often he would defer to her on some subject, playfully saying, "Well, I am not college educated as you are, and I would certainly never argue with a schoolteacher!"

He was teasing when he said this, she knew, but it was a gentle teasing, not meant to make her feel foolish or embarrassed by her strong opinions. She knew many men did not think women should voice their opinions at all, and she was glad Charles was not one of them.

The one subject upon which they did not agree, however, was venturing west. Since the husking Caroline had noticed that none of the young men talked of going west nearly as much, but occasionally the topic would come up, and Charles would speak longingly of staking a claim in one of the far-off territories.

"No trees or neighbors as far as the eye can see!" Charles would say, his whole face lighting up. "Out there a man could breathe! And never have to worry about chopping down a tree, or going too far to find meat to put on the table! When you go hunting here, there's hardly any bear or deer in the woods anymore because the place is so populated."

When Charles spoke this way, his whole demeanor changed. His eyes took on a far-away look, as if he were seeing something way in the distance and Caroline were left behind. It was a lonely feeling, and it made

her think that she and Charles were completely at odds.

This was especially true in early December, when news spread of a terrible massacre that had happened in Utah Territory earlier in the fall. According to the first newspaper reports, a group of Indians had attacked a wagon train stopped on its long journey from Arkansas to California. Every man, woman, and child had been killed. Over one hundred people!

Caroline could hardly believe it. She did not want to believe it. The very idea that so many people had been murdered sickened her. And later, when the newspapers began reporting rumors that a group of Mormons had instigated the attack, possibly even participated in the gruesome killing, Caroline was shaken to her very core.

She knew very little about Mormons, except that they worshiped differently and that some were said to take more than one wife, just as the ancient kings did in the Bible. For these reasons they had been run out of many states and had made a home for themselves in Utah. Still, Caroline could not believe a group of men who called themselves God-fearing would slaughter innocent women and children as if they were animals.

In town and at school Caroline avoided the topic as best she could. She tried not to listen when Charles and the others discussed some new piece of information from the newspapers.

"They say the wagons had stopped at a place called Mountain Meadows, and that they expected the Mormons to sell them supplies before crossing the desert," Jonah Crab said one Saturday.

"Yes, I've heard of that place. It's where wagon trains stop before they have to go across almost a hundred miles of desert," Charles added.

"That's the route I would take to California!" Henry announced.

Caroline knew he had often studied maps and talked to folks passing through Concord who were heading out to join a wagon train.

"I guess people will avoid that way for a

while!" Charlie Carpenter said.

"Wouldn't stop me!" Henry proclaimed. "I'd be ready for a fight."

"So would I!" all the young men agreed.

Caroline hated to hear them talk so. And she hated to see the boys at school making a game out of it—playing Indians and Mormons and attacking one another on a make-believe battlefield.

Sometimes she found herself imagining what it would feel like to be in a wagon train, set upon by hostile forces, with no help in sight. At those moments she was filled with a deep, cold fear and a certainty that she would never allow herself to be put in such a vulnerable position.

One Saturday the usual group of friends had gone sleighing. When talk turned to the Mountain Meadows massacre, as it was now being called, Caroline could not stand it any longer. She turned her back on the group and walked a little ways off to be alone for a moment.

"I guess it's too nice a day to talk of such

terrible things," Charles said, coming up beside her.

"Yes, it is," Caroline replied, gazing about. It *was* a lovely day. The sun was shining and the sky above the tall firs was as blue as a robin's egg. The snow sparkled like a quilt of jewels all about them.

Suddenly Caroline wondered what the fateful day had been like for those poor souls in Mountain Meadows—if there had been rain or sun. Had the weather somehow foretold their doom? For many moments Caroline strolled in silence with Charles; then she decided to be bold and say what was on her mind.

"You talk of wanting to go west," she began tentatively. "And so it could easily have been you—out there in that wagon train. What would you do if you had a wife and children to protect—or if it were your own mother and father, sisters and brothers, riding in those wagons? What could you have done in the face of such a savage attack?"

Charles's expression grew sober. "I would fight to the death to protect my family," he said in a quiet voice.

"It *would* be to the death!" Caroline found herself exclaiming. "It was for all those poor souls out there. And what would the point be? To be murdered in that way—far from family and friends? To die all alone?" Caroline stopped abruptly. She was suddenly breathless and trembling from the emotion of her words.

"I do not know why those people had to die," Charles said after a moment, seeming to choose his words carefully. "I suppose God took those folks for a purpose we cannot know here on earth."

Caroline nodded. Charles had said the right thing. It was what Mother believed as well, that God worked in mysterious ways mere mortals could not understand. Tragedy was part of life, whether Caroline liked it or not.

"All I know for sure is that those men who were headed west on that wagon train must have felt that what they were doing was right," Charles continued. "They must have felt that they would have better lives—for themselves and for their children—out there in California."

"I suppose so," Caroline said, sighing.

"That's the wonder of this great country of ours!" Charles cried. "We can make a better life for ourselves. The folks in all the countries of Europe can't do that. In those countries just a few rich men own all the land and kings and queens tell you what to do. But here we are all free and equal, and we can make something of ourselves if we have the gumption, and I guess those men out there on that wagon train had a notion to do just that. To make it better for themselves and their kin. And I believe it was noble, what they were doing, and so their death was noble too." Charles's blue eyes were aglow, and his words were spoken with such vigor, it was hard to disagree with what he was saying.

Still, she would not let herself be swayed completely. She took a deep breath and said, "It *is* noble to strive for a better life, and I admire those who voyage to unknown places. My mother did so, and her mother before her. But for myself, I am content to stay near family and friends. I am not one of those who wish to venture forth to new lands. I believe it is important to put down roots somewhere and, when the time comes, raise a family in a place where there are the benefits of education and society, not the threat of violence."

Caroline looked down at her hands clasped together in front of her. Although she felt a tension in her whole body, she was glad to have spoken her mind. Perhaps now Charles would think her a coward for wanting to stay in one place, but she wanted him to know how she truly felt.

Instead, Charles threw back his head and let out a short, loud laugh. "It is nearly impossible to argue with you!" he said, his eyes twinkling. "I can imagine what you are like in the classroom, Miss Quiner! A velvet glove covers an iron fist!"

Caroline felt the tension slip away. In truth she was not sure that Charles's assessment of her was right, but she was flattered by his words. And it was hard not to laugh when Charles was laughing.

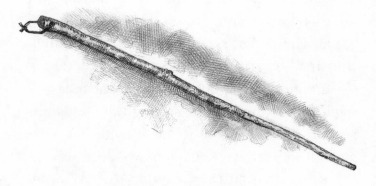

Winter Term

In the middle of December, Caroline celebrated her eighteenth birthday, and soon after that the fall term ended. There was a two-week break between terms, and that time was filled with caroling and feasting and visiting friends for Christmas and New Year's.

Caroline often found herself in the company of the Ingallses—either at their home or her own. It was clear to everyone that the two families would soon be joined, and so it made visiting even more fun. Henry had not asked Polly to marry him yet, but it seemed certain that he would.

"Perhaps there will be a double wedding between the families," Martha said to Caroline one evening as they were getting ready for bed.

"Oh, don't you start with me as well!" Caroline cried.

"Well, it's obvious how much Charles likes you," Martha persisted.

Caroline did not reply, but she wondered if it were true. The idea made her a little breathless.

"And you must like him as well," Martha continued. "You certainly have spent a lot of time with him over the past few months."

"I've spent a lot of time with all my friends," Caroline countered.

"Oh, Caroline, you know what I mean!" Martha cried in exasperation. "I've seen the way you look at him. I think you like him, too, but you won't admit it."

Now Caroline wondered about Martha's words. How did she look at Charles? She did not want to appear foolish to anyone.

"I do enjoy Charles's company, of course," Caroline said.

"Then why don't you get married!" Martha cried.

"Well, for one thing, dear sister, no one has asked me yet," Caroline replied, laughing a little.

"And what if Charles did ask you?" Martha said.

"I don't know," Caroline answered truthfully. "I would like to continue teaching school."

"Well, you can't do both," Martha said.

"I know." Caroline sighed. It was a fact that married ladies were not allowed to teach school. It did not seem fair, but Caroline knew that life was not always fair.

When the winter term started up, almost every seat in the schoolroom was taken. The older boys who had worked in fields all the rest of the year had returned to continue their learning.

Caroline felt a little jittery, as usual, on her

first day, but she was not really nervous. She knew most of the boys who were joining the class: Jim Johansen and Daniel Pike and John Paynter and the Ingalls brothers and her brother Thomas, of course. She did not anticipate any trouble from them.

There were three new boys she did not know: Dana Irving and two brothers named Caleb and Cannon Marsh. But she felt that she would be able to manage the newcomers.

Caleb and Cannon were big and burly for their age. On the first day, Caroline saw that Caleb would not be any trouble, but Cannon was a different story. The boy was bright enough, Caroline realized, but he was a lazy scholar. When he was given his first assignment to memorize and recite in class, he could remember only part of it. He made no apology, only shrugged and grinned.

"I don't know why we have to remember so many words, Miss Quiner," he said. "It seems like an awful lot."

The younger boys and girls giggled, giving Cannon courage to continue boldly, "After all, the words are always there in the books. Why can't we just read them when we feel like it? Why are we forever memorizing things?"

Caroline shushed the younger scholars, turning over in her mind what she should say. She knew she must give a good answer, an answer that would inspire everyone. Otherwise she might lose ground.

"Well, you're right, Cannon, the words are always there for us to read," Caroline said. "But memorizing passages of great works and reciting them helps keep the brain sharp. During the winter months, when your tools are not in use, you keep them oiled and sharpened, don't you?" She paused, and all the boys nodded in agreement. "Otherwise the tools get rusty and dull and are of no use at all when you need them most. It's the same with your brain. If you do not challenge yourself, your brain will stay dull."

She glanced around the room and was happy to see that all the scholars were watching her with bright, interested expressions.

She felt that she had reached everyone—everyone except Cannon.

Her heart sank a little when she saw his blank expression. He sighed and said, "I reckon I can try, for you, Miss Quiner." Then he gave her the same wide grin as before.

Cannon was a good-looking boy, with curly black hair and green eyes. He was especially handsome when he smiled, and Caroline decided that he was probably used to getting his way with a grin. So she kept her expression neutral and said in an even tone, "I would like you to do more than try, Cannon. I will need to hear you recite the whole piece tomorrow, or I will have to keep you in during recess."

Cannon's grin vanished, but he did not say anything. Caroline went on to Jim Johansen, and she was delighted when he recited the passage perfectly.

"Very good, Jim," she said.

"Thank you, Miss Quiner," Jim said.

As she turned away, Caroline thought she heard Cannon mimicking Jim, but she wasn't sure. Quickly she turned back around.

"Cannon, do you have something to recite for us now? Perhaps you have remembered it after all?"

"No, Miss Quiner," Cannon mumbled.

"All right. We must have quiet then until you are called upon," Caroline said.

The next day Caroline was relieved that Cannon did know the piece, so she did not have to punish him. But when she was ringing the bell to call the boys and girls back inside after recess, she saw Jim trip and fall in the crowd. Jim glanced around at Cannon, who was standing behind him, but he did not say anything.

"Are you all right, Jim?" Caroline asked. She was sure that Cannon had tripped the boy, but she had not actually seen him do it.

"Yes, ma'am," Jim mumbled. He would not look at her, and none of the other boys would meet her eye either. Even if they had seen something, she knew that the boys would not tattle. That was the rule of the schoolhouse. Boys and girls would never tell on one another lest they be branded tattletales.

For the rest of the week there were bits of mischief. Quill pens and pieces of chalk went missing. The clock was pushed forward an hour. And Jim and other boys would trip on their way in and out of school. Caroline was sure that Cannon was the culprit. She kept a close watch on him, but she could never catch him red-handed at anything.

"Are you having trouble at school?" Charles asked that Saturday, when they were out for a ride in the sled with the usual group.

"Why do you ask?" Caroline said in surprise.

"Jamie mentioned something about one boy making trouble, and you seem awfully quiet today," Charles answered.

"I am having a little trouble," Caroline admitted. "But it's just one boy. Last term I had some trouble in the beginning as well, but I was able to manage."

"Yes, I'm sure that you manage just fine!" Charles said.

Once more Caroline was flattered by Charles's view of her, but she wondered if she would truly be able to manage if Cannon continued his pranks. She had done well with Abe and Jack Dawson, but they were young boys. Cannon was the same age as she was, and he was much bigger. If he wanted to cause mischief, there was not much she could do about it.

During the next week, though, Caroline was determined to find a way to reach Cannon. She encouraged him when he did well and even returned his smile once or twice. The days passed smoothly, and Caroline was sure that Cannon had settled down. But the following week the pranks started up again, and then there was a fight.

Caroline was sitting at her desk with her friends during noon recess when suddenly a great shout was heard from outside. Then little Lucy Stephens came running through the door.

"Oh, Miss Quiner—it's a fight! The big boys are fighting!" she cried.

Caroline jumped up and rushed to the window. The boys had formed a circle around the yard, and two figures were in the middle, punching at each other. It was Cannon and Jim.

"Oh, Caroline—I mean Miss Quiner—what are you going to do?" Polly gasped.

Caroline did not answer. For a moment helplessness overtook her. What *could* she do? She was smaller than both Jim and Cannon. How could she possibly stop their fight? And how could she make them mind if they did not want to? If she had been a man, she could have caned them. But she was not a man. Still, she was the schoolteacher, and they must obey her.

Now Caroline's helplessness turned to anger. Jim had not caused trouble before. She was certain Cannon was the one who had started the fight.

Turning on her heel, she strode to the far corner of the room where the long thin wooden cane leaned against one wall. She had never used the cane. She had always been able to manage without it. But now she took it up and strode back down the aisle, out into the school yard.

"Teacher is here! Teacher is here!" some of

the boys yelled when they saw her.

The circle parted, and Caroline saw that Jim and Cannon were on the ground now, wrestling and grunting. There were small patches of bright-red blood in the snow around them.

For a moment she felt herself hesitate, but she made herself go forward so that she stood right over the boys.

"Stop this foolishness!" she said, but her voice sounded weak to her own ears, and the boys did not stop.

Without knowing quite what she was doing, she lifted the cane high over her head with both hands and brought it down with a loud *snap*, first on Cannon and then on Jim.

Immediately, the boys rolled away from each other and stared up at Caroline, wide-eyed.

"Get up this instant!" Caroline commanded. She was surprised how angry and strong her voice sounded now.

Jim sprang up right away, but Cannon moved more slowly, scowling and wiping at his bloodied nose.

"Take out your handkerchiefs and clean your faces," Caroline ordered in her same harsh tone.

Both boys reached into their pockets for their handkerchiefs. Cannon watched Caroline defiantly as he wiped his face, but Jim bowed his head.

"He started it," Cannon said, pointing to Jim.

"That's a lie!" Jim cried.

The boys looked as if they were about to lunge at each other again, but Caroline went to stand between them. They towered over her.

"I will have no fighting in my school," Caroline said, snapping the cane on the ground in front of her. Both boys jumped back and watched her warily.

Caroline turned and ordered the other scholars to go back into the classroom immediately. She wanted to speak to Cannon and Jim alone, though she wasn't sure what she was going to say. Desperately she wondered what punishment she should give the boys. Mr. Linney would have given them both a good caning. She had used the cane to stop the fight, but she wasn't sure she had the stomach to actually whip the boys with it.

"Jim Johansen and Cannon Marsh! I am tempted to expel both of you this instant!" Caroline said, thinking quickly as she spoke. "But I will give you one chance, and one chance only. If you are found fighting again, I will expel you for good. As for today, I am dismissing you this very minute, and you shall not come back for the rest of the week. I expect you to go straight to your homes and tell your parents why you have been dismissed. And I shall see you again come Monday."

"Yes, ma'am," Jim murmured, hanging his head.

Cannon did not say a word.

Caroline followed them back into the entryway so they could get their things. From behind the door to the schoolroom itself came footsteps and rustling, so she knew that the other scholars had gone to the window to watch.

After the boys had left, she walked back down the center aisle and put the cane back in its corner. The schoolroom was completely still. No one moved or said a word. All afternoon the scholars were quiet and obedient, and Caroline was thankful. Breaking up the fight had worn her out, and she did not think she could take another outburst.

Regrets

At four o'clock Caroline dismissed school, relieved that the day was over. John and Eliza helped tidy up as usual, and so did Thomas. Polly wanted to stay as well, but Caroline told her not to trouble herself.

After locking up the schoolhouse, Caroline set off for home with Eliza and Thomas. In town they saw the Ingallses all sitting together in their sleigh, which was tied in front of Mr. Jayson's store.

"Charles came in to go to the store, and so we're waiting for him to take us home," Polly explained. "Why don't you ride with us?"

Caroline was just about to gratefully accept the offer when she heard someone say, "Miss Quiner, I'd like to have a word with you."

She turned to find a stranger approaching her. He was about Pa's age, and there was something familiar about his face, though Caroline did not think she had met him before.

"I am Cannon's pa," the man said.

"Oh, yes," Caroline replied. Now she knew why he seemed familiar. He looked a great deal like his son.

"I want to know why you dismissed Cannon," Mr. Marsh said in a gruff voice. "I pay hard-earned money to send my boys to school."

Caroline gave an inward sigh. She was not surprised that Cannon had failed to tell his father the truth about the situation. "Well, Mr. Marsh, I am sorry to say that Cannon was fighting with another boy," she said.

Mr. Marsh scowled and shrugged just the way Cannon often did in class. "Boys will be boys," he said. "A little fighting is to be expected, I reckon. Maybe you're not cut out to handle a school. You're just a girl yourself."

Caroline's mouth opened, but no words came out. She had expected Mr. Marsh to apologize for his son's behavior, but instead he was criticizing her!

"Boys will be boys, it is true," Caroline said, lifting her chin in the air. "But there will be no fighting at my school. I explained it to Cannon. If he is caught fighting again, he will be expelled."

"Your school?" Mr. Marsh scoffed. "We'll see how long it is your school. I'll speak to Mr. Kellogg myself. A man teacher would have known what to do. He would have given them a whipping but kept them the rest of the day to learn their lessons. That's all boys need now and then to keep them in line, a good whipping. But there's no reason to send them home after the money's been paid to have them in school!"

Caroline felt her anger rising. Now she knew where Cannon had gotten his disagreeable ways. "Cannon is disrespectful and must learn a lesson, even if you will not give it to him!" she said. "Fighting disrupts everyone. Cannon will not fight at Concord School, or he shall be dismissed for good."

"Pshaw!" Mr. Marsh spluttered. "We'll see about that!" He turned in a huff and strode away.

Caroline stood watching him go. She could feel her whole body shaking now. She had spoken severely to her scholars, but never to a grown man.

"What was that all about?" Charles asked, coming up beside her.

Caroline realized that he must have seen the whole thing. She wondered if anyone else was watching, but thankfully no one was about except for her brother and sister and the other Ingallses.

"There was a fight at school today," Caroline said, sighing.

"Yes, I know—Polly told me." Charles frowned as he watched Mr. Marsh's retreating figure, then turned and reached out for Caroline's satchel. "I'll give you a ride home. Here, let me take that for you."

Caroline nodded. She felt even more tired now. She was glad Charles was there and that she wouldn't have to walk home. She wasn't sure she could make it.

Once they were rolling along Territorial Road, everyone was talking at once.

"You should have seen it, Charles!" Jamie said. "The biggest boys in the whole school were punching the living daylights out of each other—"

"And Miss Quiner went right up to them and caned them both!" Hiram finished.

"Weren't you scared?" Docia asked Caroline.

"They are just boys," Caroline answered quietly.

"They are men, really," Eliza said.

"That's true," Polly said. "Cannon is the same age as you and he certainly is a whole lot bigger. But you stepped right in between them. How brave you looked! Your eyes were flashing! Oh, Charles, you should have seen it."

"Do you think you'll have to cane them again?" Hiram asked, seeming excited by the prospect.

"I hope not," Caroline wearily replied.

The voices swirled around her for the rest of the trip home, but she did not really listen. She became aware of Charles sitting silently beside her on the wagon seat, his expression grim. Suddenly she wondered what he thought of her now. He had likened her to iron not so long ago, but she did not feel very strong this day, and she wished she had been better able to contain her emotions when she had spoken to Mr. Marsh. She was still trembling from the encounter.

When they pulled up in front of her house, Charles quickly jumped down and helped her out of the wagon seat.

"Thank you for the ride," Caroline said, smiling tentatively up at him.

Charles smacked his hat against his leg. "It makes me mad to think of that fellow talking to you like that!" he cried. "And it galls me to think of those boys disrespecting you in such a way."

Now Caroline understood that Charles was not disappointed in her at all. He was angry over what had happened.

"Maybe I could go talk some sense into those boys," Charles continued.

Caroline shook her head. "Oh, no! I must handle things myself. It would never do to have someone else step in. Then I'd never be able to keep order."

"You're right. I know it." Charles sighed. "I just wish I could be of some help."

"Thank you, Charles," Caroline said, gazing up into his eyes. "I appreciate your concern. But everything will be fine."

It was easier, she realized, to console someone else than face her own bruised pride. After she had said good-bye to Charles and was helping with the chores, she kept turning over what Mr. Marsh had said. Perhaps he was right. She was just a girl and could not manage the big boys.

"Of course Mr. Kellogg will agree with you," Mother said, once they were all seated at the supper table and Thomas and Eliza had recounted again everything that had happened.

"But perhaps I should have just whipped

them and kept them in school, as Mr. Marsh said. That's what Mr. Linney would have done," Caroline said.

"Mr. Linney might have sent them home as well," Pa said. "It sounds like that Cannon is a bad seed, from what you've told about him before. Perhaps it's best for everyone if he gets himself expelled."

The very next morning, Mr. Kellogg was waiting on the schoolhouse steps when Caroline and Eliza and Thomas arrived. Caroline was not surprised. She had expected him to come speak with her at some point during the day.

"We were all witnesses! We can tell you what happened!" Thomas said right away.

"Thank you, Thomas," Mr. Kellogg answered with a half smile. "But I don't think that will be necessary."

While Eliza swept the entryway and Thomas started the fire in the stove, Caroline explained about the fight, and then about Cannon's attitude and behavior.

"I suppose I could have simply given

Cannon and Jim a good caning and kept them here for the rest of the day," Caroline said. "But they had disrupted the other scholars quite enough already. I thought the most sensible thing would be to send them home for the rest of the week. I believe that fighting at school is serious and should be met with severe punishment."

"Of course you are right, Caroline," Mr. Kellogg said, looking thoughtful. "I do not doubt that you acted properly."

Now Caroline breathed an inward sigh of relief. She waited for what Mr. Kellogg would say next.

"I am afraid this Cannon sounds like a problem, though," Mr. Kellogg continued, "and I wonder if you'll be able to make him mind you. Perhaps I could, as head of the school board, step in if needed."

"Thank you, Mr. Kellogg," Caroline said, "but I would like to try to handle it myself first."

"All right, then," Mr. Kellogg replied. "I will tell Mr. Marsh that the school board upholds your decision. The boys will stay out the rest of the week. I trust you will keep me apprised of the situation."

Mr. Kellogg took his leave, and Caroline stood for a moment in quiet contemplation. She was glad Mr. Kellogg had agreed with her, but it made her squirm a little to think of how angry Mr. Marsh would be when he heard the news. She wondered if he would keep Cannon out of school altogether. She hoped not. Even though Cannon was a problem, she hated to give up so easily. Every boy or girl deserved the chance to learn, and she was determined to help Cannon no matter what.

The rest of the week was quiet and uneventful. The following Monday morning Caroline was eager to see how Cannon and Jim would behave when they arrived.

Jim came to school early. His face was still a little bruised and scratched, and his nose was swollen at the bridge.

"I'm mighty sorry about the other day, ma'am," Jim said, holding his hat in his hands.

"I'm surprised at you, Jim," Caroline said.

Jim looked down at the floor.

"You are one of the oldest in the class, and you are one of my best scholars," Caroline continued. "I expect you to set a good example for the others, and that means no fighting."

"Yes, ma'am," Jim said.

Caroline told Jim to change his seat so that he would not be sitting next to Cannon anymore. He took his books and put them in the second-to-last row.

Soon the shoolroom began to fill. Cannon and Caleb arrived very close to nine o'clock. Cannon took his seat right away without coming to make any apology to Caroline.

Caroline steeled herself for a difficult day. All morning she waited for some kind of mischief, but none came. When she called on the older boys, she was not surprised that Cannon did not know any of his recitation.

"How could I, Miss Quiner?" he asked, giving Caroline his grin. "You sent me home."

"Your brother, Caleb, should have given you your assignments," Caroline answered.

Caleb darted a look at Cannon but did not say anything. Caroline suspected that Caleb had given him the assignments but Cannon had chosen not to learn them.

"Very well, you will have two whole pages to learn by tomorrow, not just one," Caroline said.

The next day Cannon still could not recite the whole assignment. He stumbled over the word *dissension* and then stopped completely.

"How can we be expected to say such big words when we don't know what they mean, Miss Quiner?" he asked.

"If you don't know the meaning of a word, you may look it up in the dictionary, Cannon," Caroline answered as pleasantly as she could.

"We ain't got no dictionary at home," Cannon said.

"It may be that you *do not have* a dictionary at home," Caroline automatically corrected. "But there is a dictionary here, for anyone to use."

Cannon did not have anything to say to that. Caroline rose up from her desk and beckoned to him. "Come, let us look up the word together."

Cannon noisily got up from his seat and trudged, scowling, to the teacher's desk. He stood over Caroline as she paged through the dictionary.

"Please read the word and definition out loud," Caroline said when they had come to the right page.

Cannon slowly read, "'Dissension: disagreement that gives rise to strife.'"

Caroline smiled to herself. She wondered if Cannon had actually chosen to stumble over a word that aptly described what was happening between them, but he didn't seem to grasp the irony of his choice. He simply looked bored.

"Thank you, Cannon. You may sit down now," Caroline said, and Cannon shrugged and went back to his seat.

They moved on to arithmetic. She set the older scholars to working on their long division. The younger ones she brought forward to recite their multiplication tables out loud.

The class was just coming to the end of the lesson when a loud *hiss* was heard, followed by a *crash* and a great *splat!* The whole room erupted into giggles.

Right away Caroline knew what had happened. Someone had set a corked ink bottle on the hot stove. The heat had made the bottle explode. Ink was now dripping from the ceiling and running down the sides of the stove. It was an old schoolboy prank, but one that had not happened thus far while Caroline had been teaching.

Caroline brought the school to order. "Who did this?" she demanded, knowing full well that no one would answer, and knowing, too, that Cannon was most likely the culprit.

She walked down the rows, glancing from desk to desk. Only the older scholars had ink bottles. The younger ones worked with chalk and slates. She noticed that Jim's ink bottle was missing.

"Jim, was that your ink bottle?" she asked in a gentle voice.

"Yes, ma'am," he answered. His face was red, and he would not meet her eye.

Caroline was sure that Jim had not placed the ink bottle on the stove himself, but she had no choice but to ask him to clean up the mess, since it was his. And she had to make him stay after school to help clean the blackboard as punishment as well.

Over the next few days Cannon did not do anything himself, but Abe and Jack Dawson were back to their old tricks. They pinned Lucy Stephens's braids to the back of her chair with a pocketknife, and they drew cartoons of the other scholars on their slates and passed them around.

Whenever Caroline caught them at any mischief, she noticed how pleased Cannon looked. She suspected that he was egging them on, but she could not prove it.

Day by day the mischief continued and Caroline grew more angry and frustrated. At times she wanted to cry, and at other times she wanted to give Cannon the whipping he deserved. But she resolved to be calm and collected always, no matter what she felt inside. She knew Cannon wanted some kind of reaction from her, and she did not want to give him the satisfaction.

Then one day after recess Caroline noticed that John Friday was limping a little as he came in from playing outside.

"What happened, John?" she asked.

"Nothing, ma'am," John mumbled.

Caroline glanced up and caught sight of Cannon nearby. He was making a face at John, but he stopped as soon as he knew Caroline was watching.

"Did someone hurt you on the playground, John?" she asked in a quiet voice.

John shook his head and murmured, "No, ma'am. I tripped is all."

Caroline glanced again at Cannon, but he had looked away.

The next day John came back from recess with a tear in his coat. It was a new coat that Mr. Kellogg had bought for him for Christmas, and Caroline knew that John was very proud of it.

"What happened to your coat, John?" Caroline gently asked.

"I tore it," he said, but he would not meet her eye.

"How did you do that?" Caroline persisted.

"I caught it on the thornbush," he said.

Again Caroline saw that Cannon was smirking in the back of the room. It was terrible to think of such a big boy picking on someone half his age and size. She knew that John would never speak up out of pride, but she hoped that some of the other boys would come to John's aid.

"Everybody knows John is your pet," Thomas said that evening when Caroline prodded him. "I haven't seen it myself, but I think Cannon is picking on him when he knows no one is looking."

"What a bully!" Caroline exclaimed. She was shocked that Cannon would be so malicious.

The next day she vowed to be vigilant and keep a sharp eye out during morning recess and at noontime. She did not eat with her friends but went outside instead and walked about the school yard.

Nothing happened that day or the next, but one afternoon she had to stay inside to help two little girls with their grammar. When it was nearly time to ring the bell, Caroline heard a commotion, and she rushed outside to find Cannon and Jim fighting again.

Mother had always taught her that young ladies never yell, but suddenly Caroline was doing just that.

"Stop! Stop this instant!"

The boys froze and stared at her. Everyone in the school yard was staring.

"I warned you boys! I expected you to cause trouble again, Cannon Marsh, but I am especially disappointed in you, Jim Johansen!" she exclaimed.

Cannon watched her defiantly, but Jim hung his head. Then John Friday came tentatively forward.

"Jim was fighting on account of me, Miss Quiner," he said in a near whisper. "He stepped in when Cannon was picking on me, and Cannon wouldn't let it go."

Caroline looked at Jim. "Is this true?"

Jim did not answer.

"It is true." Thomas came forward, and so

did the Ingalls boys. They all said that Cannon was being a bully, and that Jim had just tried to protect John Friday.

Caroline was proud of the boys for breaking the schoolhouse rule of no tattling. She gave them all a smile of approval, then turned to face Cannon. "I gave you a fair warning. Now I have no recourse but to expel you from Concord School for good."

"I'm sick and tired of you and this old school anyway," Cannon yelled. "Come on, Caleb!" He turned and stalked away without bothering to get his things from the schoolhouse. Caleb looked as though he wanted to say something to Caroline, but then he silently followed his brother.

Caroline told everyone to go back inside. Then she spoke with Jim alone.

"I still do not approve of fighting, no matter what the reason," Caroline said. "I'm afraid I will have to punish you for that. But I do appreciate what you did for someone younger and smaller than yourself."

Jim nodded and gave a faint half smile.

Caroline told him to get his things and go home for the rest of the day.

"I will speak to Mr. Kellogg about what's to be done," she said.

The next morning Mr. Kellogg appeared before school. He told her that he would need to interview Jim and some of the other boys as well, since Mr. Marsh had lodged a complaint about her.

Caroline had expected no less, but she waited anxiously for a full week for the mess to be sorted out. Finally, Mr. Kellogg told her that the board had reached a decision. They had upheld Cannon's expulsion and decided that Jim could stay, but he was on probation. As punishment, he must help Caroline with any chores before and after school for the rest of the term.

One Saturday after the whole thing had blown over, Caroline was riding in the sleigh with Charles and her friends.

"I guess you're glad how things turned out," Charles said to her.

"No, not really," Caroline answered.

"What do you mean?" Charles asked in surprise.

"Well, I wish that Mr. Marsh had not taken Caleb out of school as well. He was a good scholar, and it's a shame he has to pay the price for his brother's bad behavior." Caroline paused. "And I wish I had been able to reach Cannon and show him how wonderful learning can be."

"I guess some folks are beyond reach," Charles said.

Caroline was quiet. She knew Charles was trying to say the right thing. The life of a teacher must be full of ups and downs and regrets, she guessed, though she could not help but feel she had failed a little with Cannon Marsh, and she did so wish that things had turned out differently.

Good-bye

Winter had come early that year, and thankfully spring did the same. By the middle of March the snow had melted away completely, leaving the fields dark and bare, ready for plowing.

One by one the big boys dropped out of school before the term was finished. Caroline could not blame them, though she was disappointed that they would not finish all their lessons. She knew they were needed to help with the work at home now that winter was over.

Good-bye

Caroline wanted to graduate Jim that year, but she was unable to do so, since he was dropping out early as well. He came to speak with her on his last day.

"I am sorry, Miss Quiner, but I've got to work with Pa," Jim said. "I will still come to help you before and after school, though."

"That won't be necessary, Jim," Caroline said. "You are released from your duties. I am proud of what you've accomplished this term after the trouble with Cannon. You are a good scholar. I hope you come back next year, and then I will graduate you."

"Are you going to be the teacher next year?" Jim asked, looking surprised.

"Why wouldn't I be?" Caroline replied.

Jim's cheeks turned bright pink, and he stammered, "Oh, I'm sorry, Miss Quiner, I don't mean to be impertinent. I just always see you with Charles Ingalls, and I thought you would get hitched like all the other young ladies seem to be doing."

Caroline felt her own cheeks coloring. She knew that Jim's older sister Hannah was getting "hitched." And just that week, Jonah and Elmira had become engaged, and so had Lucy and Samuel. Caroline did not think that Henry and Polly would be far off, and neither would Maddy and her Cyrus.

"No, Jim, I am not engaged, and I do expect to graduate you next year," Caroline said, smiling.

"Yes, ma'am!" Jim replied, returning her smile.

Now that it was spring, the Saturday outings stopped. Springtime was the busiest season, next to fall. The young men spent long hours getting the fields ready for planting. Couples saw each other at church on Sundays, and some went for drives together afterward.

When Charles began asking Caroline to drive with him after church on Sundays in his pa's buggy, she happily accepted, though she couldn't help but wonder what the drives meant. Charles seemed to go out of his way to spend time with her, yet he still talked of going west.

One Sunday, after the winter term had

ended and before the spring term began, Charles asked to see Caroline home from church as usual. The sky was blue, and a spring breeze gently tugged at Caroline's bonnet strings as she rode in the buggy. Beside her Charles seemed to be in a particularly good mood, his eyes dancing as he sent the horse trotting past slower drivers on Territorial Road.

After they had turned into the woods, Charles drove to a quiet spot and brought the buggy to a halt.

"I wanted to show you this," he said, reaching into his pocket and bringing out a folded piece of paper. "Mr. Jayson just got these notices yesterday. It's about free land in Dakota Territory."

Caroline's heart sank as she watched Charles smooth out the paper.

"Free land! Can you imagine!" Charles cried, his face aglow with excitement. "All a man has to do is stake his claim and stay there for five years, and then the place is his, free and clear!"

Caroline pretended to study the notice, though in truth she was not really seeing it. Her eyes could not seem to focus. "So you plan to go there? To Dakota Territory?" she asked in a small voice.

"A man can hardly pass up such an opportunity as this!" Charles said. He gazed at the notice for a moment and then began to speak in a rush. "Of course I couldn't make it out this spring. I have to go this week and help Peter put in the crops, and he'll give me a share of the profits. I hope we'll make some money over the next few months, hauling lumber like we did last year. But I should be able to head out come fall. It's important to get settled someplace well before the winter sets in."

"Yes, it's important to get settled," Caroline echoed. She did not think what she said mattered anyway. Charles was still sitting beside her, but already he seemed very far away.

He started talking again in a rush, telling all he knew about the land in the Dakota Territory. Caroline listened to the tone of his

Good-bye

voice—how happy he sounded!—but she could not seem to concentrate on what he was saying. She felt as though her corset strings were pulled too tight, because she could not seem to catch her breath.

"A man can walk a day and not meet another soul," Charles said.

Caroline looked down at her gloved hands clasped together in her lap and made herself breathe steadily. She had been waiting for this moment all along—the moment when Charles would announce that he was leaving. She should have been ready for it, but she was not. Suddenly she knew for certain: She did not want Charles to go.

"What do you think?" Charles asked then.

Caroline made herself raise her chin and look at Charles. How confident he appeared, the sunlight playing across his handsome face, how capable and sure. She did not want him to go, but neither would she hold him back from following his dream.

"It certainly does seem like an opportunity that's hard to pass up," Caroline replied in an

291

even tone. "I think you should do it. You've always talked of wanting to go out there. And there's no time like the present, as they say."

"You're right at that!" Charles cried, smiling. "No time like the present!" He gazed down at the notice in his hands and then carefully folded the paper and tucked it back inside his jacket pocket.

"I could send for you, once I get settled," Charles said in a quiet voice. He did not look at her but kept his eyes on some far-off point. "It might take a year, but I'm sure I could make it comfortable for you out there. It's not as rough as Kansas, I hear. There's hardly a soul out there, so there's no fighting."

For a moment Caroline felt a fluttering, as if a butterfly were somehow trapped inside her chest, beating its tiny wings. Charles was asking her to join him! All she had to do was say yes!

But she could not. Something held her back. She wanted to think it was instinct or common sense. Perhaps it was only cowardice. Whatever it was, she knew she did not want to go to Dakota Territory—a place where a man could walk a day without seeing a soul. She had not forgotten the fear she had felt after hearing about the terrible events of the Mountain Meadows massacre. And she had not forgotten the things she had said to Charles way back in December, but apparently he had.

Or maybe he did remember, and he was just giving her a polite way out of a delicate situation. Maybe he knew already that she would say no to his offer. If so, it was best to get things settled quickly.

Caroline made her voice sound light and cheerful. "So much can happen in a year! You will be busy and so will I! Mr. Kellogg mentioned to me recently that there are more settlers each day in Concord, and so there will be many more scholars in need of education. He is counting on me to run the school. And I cannot let him down."

Caroline stopped abruptly. She did not want to have to say another word, but Charles was strangely silent, watching her, and she made herself go brightly on. "I have so enjoyed the time we have spent together, Charles. You are such good company and we have had many lively debates. And of course I wish you the very best in everything that you do. I know you will succeed out there, or anywhere else you may go. . . ." Her words trailed off. She suddenly felt very tired and she wanted to be home, alone in her room.

"I see," Charles said.

Caroline could not look at him—otherwise she would change her mind, and she was suddenly convinced that an engagement was something neither of them really wanted.

"I'll take you home then," Charles said in a voice she could not read. He took up the reins and called, "Giddyap," sending the horse trotting through the sunny woods.

All about, the birds were gaily singing. Caroline usually loved to hear the joyful sound, but today it seemed to her that the birds were mocking her with their happy song.

Finally the buggy rolled into the clearing and Charles brought them to a halt. Caroline was relieved to see that no one was about. Perhaps Pa had taken Mother and the others for a Sunday drive as well.

Charles came around to help her to the ground. They stood for a moment in silence. Then Charles said, "I guess this is good-bye, then. I'll be heading to Peter's tomorrow, and then I'll be busy all summer getting ready to go."

"Yes, Charles." Caroline made herself smile. "Good-bye and good luck!"

Charles jumped back onto the buggy seat, took hold of the reins, and with a wave was gone.

Caroline wanted to turn and go inside the house, but she could not move. She felt rooted to the spot. She watched the place where Charles had disappeared into the woods. Her eyes filled with tears, and angrily she wiped them away. She had made the right decision, she was sure. And so there was no reason at all to cry.

My Heart Is Sair

Caroline had told Charles she would be busy, and so she was. It was true that many new families had settled around Concord, and so summer school was more crowded than it had been the previous year, though none of Caroline's own friends were attending. They were all engaged now, busy with sewing quilts and gowns and linens for their lives as married ladies. This was true of Polly as well.

Henry had finally asked Polly to marry him, and she had said yes. They would wait until the following winter, after Henry had built her a house on the plot of land he shared with Joseph.

So Henry would not be venturing off after all! Love and impending marriage had made him decide to stay put for a while. Caroline was amazed by this abrupt change in attitude. And even though she was thrilled that Polly, who had always been her good friend, would soon be her sister, she could not help but feel a tinge of sadness at the turn of events.

What if she had had the nerve to ask Charles to stay—would he have done it? This was the question her mind kept returning to as she went about her chores and her school-work.

No, she did not think so. She remembered how excited Charles had been when talking about Dakota Territory. She did not think anything would have swayed his determination.

So, what if she had had the courage to say yes to his proposal? Perhaps she was just being stubborn in her adamant refusal to leave Concord.

But if she left, she might never see her family again. Mother had come west, and even though she talked of returning to Boston one day to see Grandma and Grandpa Tucker, Caroline doubted that she ever would. Boston was very far away, and it cost so much to travel such a great distance.

It made Caroline's heart ache to think of leaving Mother and Pa and her brothers and sisters. But it was terrible to think of never seeing Charles again.

My heart is sair.

The words came to her suddenly one rainy summer day as she tidied up the schoolhouse after everyone else had left.

My heart is sair, I dare na tell,
My heart is sair for Somebody.

It was the song Charles had played at the cornhusking. Caroline knew that "sair" was the Scottish way of saying "sore." The lyrics described her perfectly. Her heart was yearning for Charles, yet she could not tell anyone of her true feelings. She had revealed to no one what had happened that spring day when Charles had said good-bye. Polly and Martha and Eliza had all tried to pry it out of her at one time or another, but Caroline had said only that Charles had decided to go away, nothing more.

Now the strange melody that Charles had played way back in the fall haunted Caroline as she went about her daily routine. Most of the time she was not even aware of humming it out loud, but one evening Mother remarked upon it.

"Why, I have not heard that song in years!" she cried, rising up from a garden row. She and Caroline were alone together, doing the weeding. Eliza and Lottie had gone to fetch the cows, and Martha was working at Widow Milton's.

"Do you know that song?" Caroline asked.

"Yes, it was a favorite of Grandma Tucker's. She used to sing it when I was young,"

Mother said, pausing in her work and stretching herself up to a kneeling position.

"Did you use to sing it to us?" Caroline asked, sitting back on her knees.

"I suppose so," Mother said thoughtfully. "But I have not thought of it in so long! The words are by the Scottish poet Robert Burns. He was one of Mama's favorite poets when she was a young girl in Scotland, and she often used to quote his poems to us." Mother was quiet for a time, remembering. Then she tentatively sang a few words and Caroline joined in. When they finished, Mother shivered. "Goodness, what a sad song it is, now that I think about it!"

"Charles played it at the cornhusking, when we were all getting ready for sleep," Caroline said. She bent down to get back to work pulling weeds, but when she glanced up, she realized that Mother was watching her with a quizzical expression on her face.

"Did Charles say when he would return?" Mother asked.

Caroline shook her head. "I expect he'll come back long enough to settle his affairs.

Then he'll head off to Dakota Territory."

"Did he ask you to go with him?"

Caroline grew warm all over, and she could not meet Mother's eye. No one had posed the question so directly. Caroline did not really want to answer, but she knew she could not lie to Mother.

"He offered to send for me," Caroline said at last.

"And what did you say?"

"I told him I did not want to go," Caroline said quietly, and then suddenly she cried, "Oh, Mother, I wonder if I have made a terrible mistake!"

"Tell me all about it," Mother said in her kind, gentle voice, exactly as she had always done when Caroline was a little girl with some problem that seemed impossible to solve, a terrible weight upon her shoulders. Mother had always, with a hug and a kiss and a word of wisdom, been able to make everything all right.

And now Caroline again desperately wanted Mother to make everything all right.

She revealed how she had felt when she had first seen Charles again after so many years, and her growing feelings for him once they had spent more time together. She described how smart and thoughtful he was and how much they seemed to enjoy one another's company. Then she talked about her own fears of going west, and Charles's determination to do just that.

When at last she ran out of words, she simply sat, head bowed, waiting to hear what Mother would say.

"My dear, you have not changed much since you were a little girl. You always pondered things so deeply and held your worries in until you were near to bursting." Mother sighed. Then she asked, "Caroline, do you love Charles?"

Caroline was shocked by the direct question. "Oh, Mother, I want to continue to be a schoolteacher and help you and Pa. . . ."

"You have helped us quite a bit already, Caroline, so do not worry yourself about that," Mother said, brushing a hand in the air.

"Besides, I did not ask you if you wanted to keep teaching. I asked if you love Charles Ingalls."

"Yes, I do," Caroline said, and it was as though a weight were being lifted from her chest. She had admitted being in love to no one, not even herself. But now that she had said it out loud, she felt lighter somehow. "But . . . but . . . but . . ." she stammered, confused. "It does not seem very practical! When I look at it like an arithmetic problem, it is easy to understand. Charles wants one thing and I want another, and the two things do not add up."

Mother shook her head, laughing. She reached a hand out to gently tuck a loose strand of hair behind Caroline's ear. "Love is not always practical, Caroline. You are such a bright young woman, but sometimes you must listen to your heart, not just to your head."

Caroline was surprised at Mother's words. She mulled them over for a moment and then asked, "Is that what you did with Father?"

"Oh, yes," Mother answered, nodding. "I

was very much in love with Mr. Henry Quiner. When he smiled, it seemed to me that all was right with the world." Mother gazed off into the distance. "I too did not think I wanted to give up my work as a dressmaker. I certainly did not like the idea of leaving Boston. But once I had put my hand into his, I knew I would follow him to the ends of the earth, if that was where he wanted to go."

Caroline watched her mother's wistful face. It was strange and wonderful to try to imagine her as a young woman, so in love she was willing to leave everything behind. In the years after Father's death, there had been so much hardship, Mother had become very practical. She was rarely frivolous in any way.

Still, something made Caroline hold back from embracing all that Mother said. "But if you had not come west, if you had persuaded Father to stay in Boston, perhaps he would not have had to go off on a trading ship to earn extra wages for the family. Perhaps he would still be alive today."

"Caroline, we cannot live our lives worrying about 'what if'!" Mother said emphatically. "Grandma Tucker would never have had the courage to leave Scotland and make the perilous voyage to this country if she had worried about what *might* happen. And I would never have journeyed west myself. Then I would never have had the joy of raising eight wonderful children."

"There has been a great deal of sorrow with the joy," Caroline said in a quiet voice.

"Yes," Mother replied, sighing again. "But perhaps the joy would not seem so sweet without the sorrow." Mother's gaze focused intently on Caroline again. "Sorrow and joy are both a part of life, Caroline. And life is what we choose to make of it."

At that moment, Eliza and Lottie came out of the woods, leading the cow and her calf, and so Caroline and Mother silently went back to work. For the rest of the evening Caroline was quiet, pondering Mother's words.

That night she lay awake in bed for a long while beside her sleeping sisters, listening to the sounds of the night. A lone wolf was howling far off in the distance. The cicadas were buzzing in the dark, and the hoot owl was calling from his hole in the old oak tree at the edge of the clearing.

Who? Who? he called, and it seemed to Caroline he was directing the question just to her.

Who, who do you love?

Charles Ingalls was the answer. Caroline knew it for certain. But what did it matter now? She had already told him good-bye.

A Right Pretty Spot

J uly came and went. Caroline looked for Charles at the Independence Day festivities in Concord, but he was not there. Polly mentioned that he and Peter were very busy, working the land and hauling lumber. Mr. Fleming and Mr. Biles played the fife and drum again, but there was no fiddling, and many people remarked upon the need to find another fiddler to take Charles's place.

For her own part Caroline doubted she would ever find someone to fill the void left in her heart by Charles. Still, she would not let herself wallow in self-pity. She finished the summer term and busied herself around the farm as usual. In late August she took on more sewing work for Mr. Jayson, and she happily attended the wedding celebrations of her friends Jonah and Elmira and Samuel and Lucy.

In early September, she heard at last the news she supposed she had been waiting for all along: Charles had come home.

She assumed he would help his father with some of the fall harvest and then set off on his journey west. She knew it was inevitable that their paths would cross at some point during his time in Concord. Perhaps she would run into him at Mr. Jayson's store, or at church on a Sunday.

And so she prepared herself as best she could for these meetings. Imaginary conversations swirled around inside her head.

At first she envisioned telling Charles that she had made a mistake, that she would wait for him to send for her after all, if that was what he still wanted. But how could she know if that was what he truly wanted? And how could she be so bold and freely speak her mind in such a way, laying her heart bare before him?

She was not that brave—she knew it for a fact. And she practiced the more probable conversations they might have, conversations that revolved around the weather and family news and good-bye.

That very Sunday, Caroline was sitting in the church pew with her family when suddenly Eliza's elbow dug into her ribs.

"Eliza! That hurt!" Caroline cried in a whisper.

"It's Charles! He's here!" Eliza whispered, leaning in close.

Caroline did not turn to look, but her heart began to race. Once the singing had started and they were all standing, she did turn a little. Charles was at the end of the row, next to his pa. He had the hymnbook open before him and he was singing, but his blue eyes were watching her! He gave a tentative half smile, and Caroline could not help it. She smiled back.

After the hymn was over, they all sat again and Reverend Jones began his sermon, but

A Little House of Their Own

Caroline did not hear any of it that day. Her thoughts were tangled, wondering what Charles's smile could possibly mean. When it was time to stand and sing again, she automatically did so, but she could not have said later what hymns were played.

At last church was over, and the congregation filed out the doors and spilled into the dusty street. The day was warm and humid for September, and the sun shone brightly overhead. Caroline was glad she had worn her light silk dress with the low collar. But she fumbled a little with her bonnet strings, which had seemed too tight all through church.

Eliza had stuck to her side as they came out the door, and now she grabbed Caroline's arm and squeezed. "Charles is coming this way!" she whispered.

Caroline took a deep breath. If this was the moment of their final good-bye, she wanted to get it over with as quickly and smoothly as possible.

"Hello, Charles!" Eliza called as he came up beside them and tipped his hat.

"Good day, Eliza," Charles said in a cheerful voice. "Good day, Caroline."

"Good day, Charles," Caroline replied, glancing tentatively up into his face.

"A fine summer we've had," Charles said.

"Yes, it has been a fine summer," Caroline replied.

"Not too hot and plenty of rain."

"We've been very lucky indeed."

"Your family is well, I trust?" Charles asked.

"Oh, yes, we are all quite well, thank you," Caroline answered.

This was exactly like the conversations she had rehearsed. It would probably last a few brief moments, and then it would be thankfully over, and she would never see Charles again.

"Caroline," Charles began, and then he stopped and cleared his throat. "I was wondering . . . if you would mind taking a drive with me."

"A d-d-d-drive?" Caroline asked, stammering. She was not sure she had heard him correctly. She had not rehearsed this scene at all.

Charles nodded. He looked down at the

ground and kicked at something with his boot. "If you have the time for a drive."

"Oh, I am certain she has the time!" Eliza said, squeezing Caroline's arm even tighter. "We have nothing planned at all today, of course, since it is Sunday. Isn't that right, Caroline?"

Caroline hesitated, glancing from Eliza to Charles. He seemed unsure, waiting for an answer. She nodded, not trusting her own voice.

Eliza let go of her arm, and Charles took her lightly by the elbow just as he used to do, guiding her through the crowd.

As he helped her up onto the buggy seat, Caroline caught sight of Mother standing near Pa's wagon. Mother smiled and nodded, and in a daze of confusion Caroline nodded back.

Charles hopped up beside Caroline, and soon they were driving down Main Street and onto Territorial Road. They waved to friends and neighbors as they passed. Some called out, "Hello, Ingalls! Welcome back!"

Charles turned off into the woods at the usual spot and headed back toward the Ingalls cabin. Caroline grew curious, wondering where he was taking her. She wanted to ask, but she still did not trust herself to speak.

Charles turned again and followed the creek for a time, until they had come to a place where a few trees had obviously been cleared in recent days. The dozen or so stumps sticking up from the ground were yellowish green where they had been cut, and the logs had been rolled to one side.

"Here we are," Charles said, tugging at the reins and jumping down to tether the horse to a tree. He quickly strode around the buggy and held out a hand to Caroline.

Wordlessly, she let herself be helped down and led to the middle of the little clearing.

"What do you think?" Charles asked, turning in a full circle.

"What do I think?" Caroline repeated the question, unsure what the answer should be.

"See, the creek runs nearby, the land dips a little, so that a person has a nice view of the hills over yonder. But there's also plenty of flat land for planting," Charles said. "I always thought this was a right pretty place."

"It is a pretty place," Caroline agreed, feeling confused.

"I used to come here when we first moved to these parts," Charles continued. "I liked practicing my fiddle here, where no one could hear me."

"I heard you practicing," Caroline said in a quiet voice. "Do you remember? Henry and I came upon you once. At first I thought it was the trees singing."

"I remember," Charles answered softly. Then he grinned. "I'm glad you like it, 'cause Pa said I could have it if I clear it and work it myself."

"Oh!" Caroline cried. "But what about Dakota Territory and all that free land?"

Charles shrugged. "There's plenty of good land around here, I reckon."

Caroline was speechless, and her heart was beating so loudly now, she was sure that Charles would be able to hear it.

"Aw, I guess it made me mad at first, when you told me good-bye," Charles said, studying her face as he spoke. "I thought you were just being coy. But I knew that wasn't like you. And then I thought about what you said last winter. I know you feel strongly about staying in one place, and I'm willing to try it for a while."

Charles paused to remove his hat. Then he took a deep breath and said, "I can't promise I'll always stay in one place, Caroline. But I'd like to try my luck here for a bit. I would like to build a house for you in these woods. That is, if you'll let me."

Caroline thought her heart might burst, it was beating so very quickly inside her chest. She turned to gaze about the tiny clearing, and many images came to her at once. She saw the tattered ribbon little John Friday had given her and she recalled the look of wonder on the boy's face when he had finally learned to read. She hated the idea of giving up being a schoolteacher, but she hated more the idea of giving up the man she loved.

Love was not like an arithmetic problem at all, she suddenly decided. There was no simple answer. And life was what we chose to make of it, just as Mother had said.

"Yes, Charles," Caroline answered, turning back to him.

"You mean it?" he asked, his whole face lighting up.

Caroline nodded, knowing her own face was glowing with happiness. "Yes, Charles, I do."

Charles grinned and slapped his hat against his thigh. Then his expression grew sober. He reached out to take her hands in his own and leaned down to gently kiss her.

"It will be a little house at first," Charles said after a moment, his voice sounding gruff with emotion. "But it will be a solid house, I promise you that, Caroline! It will be a little house of our own."

"I don't mind a little house," Caroline said, knowing in her heart it was true.

It did not matter how big or small the house. And it no longer even mattered where the house happened to be—either near to Concord or far, far away. Home is where the heart is, the old saying went. And Caroline knew, deep in her bones, that her heart would always be with Charles Ingalls.

Epilogue

*I*n 1860 Caroline Quiner and Charles Ingalls
were married in Concord, Wisconsin. The couple
knew that many adventures lay ahead of them, and
they were eager for a family and a little house of
their own. What they did not know was that they
were destined to become one of the most celebrated
pioneer families in American history.

This was the second time a Quiner had married
an Ingalls, and it would not be the last. Caroline's
brother Henry had married Charles's sister Polly
two years earlier, and Caroline's sister Eliza
would marry Charles's brother Peter just a year
later. And when many of Charles's family members
packed up and headed north to Pepin, Wisconsin,
Caroline and Charles gladly joined them.

Together with Henry and Polly Quiner,
Caroline and Charles bought eighty acres of land
and built two little log cabins. Against the back-
drop of the Civil War, Caroline and Charles began
their life together. But the war seemed far away

from the quiet lives of the pioneers in the Big Woods, who spent their busy days farming and making a home.

Caroline and Charles worked hard on their farm, and in 1865 Caroline gave birth to their first child, Mary. Then, in 1867, in the little house on the Wisconsin farm in the Big Woods, their second daughter, Laura, was born, and the beloved story of the famous little pioneer girl began. Laura grew up to become Laura Ingalls Wilder, and decades later she recorded her pioneer experiences growing up on the prairie, preserving for generations to come a magnificent record of days gone by.